GUIDEPOSTS

The Greedy Auctioneer

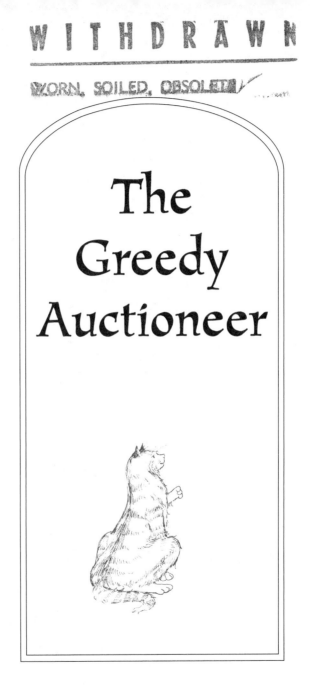

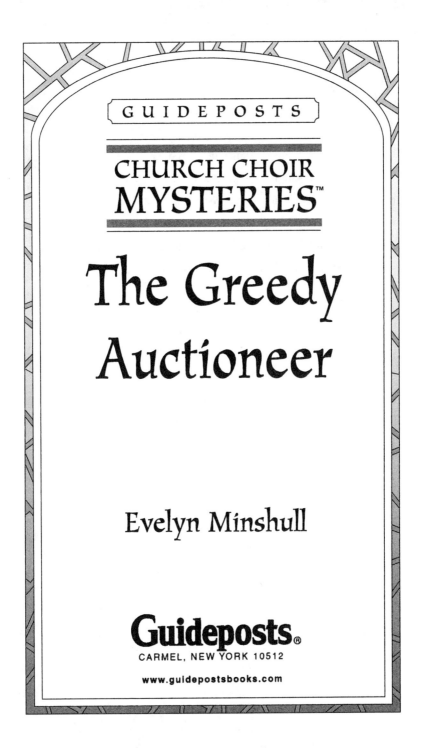

GUIDEPOSTS

CHURCH CHOIR
MYSTERIES™

The Greedy
Auctioneer

Evelyn Minshull

Guideposts®

CARMEL, NEW YORK 10512

www.guidepostsbooks.com

www.guidepostsbooks.com
Series Editor: Michele Slung
Cover art by Stephen Gardner & Edgar Jerins
Cover design by Wendy Bass
Interior design by José R. Fonfrias
Interior cat illustrations by Viqui Maggio
Typeset by Composition Technologies, Inc.
Printed in the United States of America

For Amy Jenkins, Ellen Cohen, Robin Hittie, Jean Allen
and Shirley Kougher—
who conspire to inspire organization.

Acknowledgments

WHILE DESIGNING this further adventure of Gracie Lynn Parks and crew, I revisited, reappraised and rediagnosed a most grievous character affliction—my paralysis by clutter. Therefore, I would like to acknowledge the following:

- With compassion—those who, like me, wrestle with this malady.
- With infinite gratitude—those who love (or at least endure) us despite our flaws.
- With profound respect (verging envy)—those who by some alchemy *combine* creativity and organization, and so liberate the remainder of humanity from chaos.

Chief of these last would be Pamela Bloom, Elizabeth Kramer Gold, Michele Slung and Stephanie Castillo Samoy. These remarkable women have given birth to Willow Bend and its delightful cast of main characters; selected, coordinated and encouraged the various authors; and infused character, setting and voice with coherence and consistency. Unreservedly, I applaud you!

More than I can express, I enjoy being a part of the Willow Bend family!

The
Greedy
Auctioneer

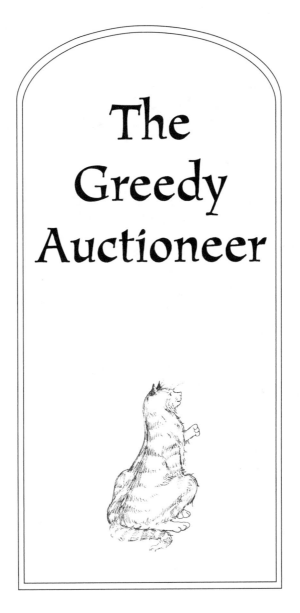

GRACIE LYNN PARKS PAUSED at the open oven door as the pounding two stories overhead intensified. *Dear Lord,* she prayed inwardly, *please don't let him damage himself.*

She was grateful that her octogenarian uncle refused to take to a rocking chair and grumble about the osteoarthritis that often forced him to use a walker. *But there has to be a happy medium, doesn't there, Lord—between vegetating, waiting for death—and inviting it by self-inflicted mutilation?* Earlier, he'd husked a bushel of black walnuts, then smashed the shells, his mallet thudding in staccato. Presenting the meats with a pleased expression and blackened hands, he'd suggested, "Aunt Alice's special cake?" and had promptly gone to fix the broken porch rail. Gracie had cringed at each shriek of the electric drill.

Marge Lawrence—Gracie's neighbor and best friend—set her mug on the tabletop, sloshing tea. "Sorry." Her cluster of bracelets jangled. "But what on earth is that man doing up there? And how do you survive it?"

Gracie spooned brown sugar and butter topping over a dozen apple dumplings and closed the oven door before answering. "He's hunting for forgotten treasure to put in the Eternal Hope auction. And how do I survive it?" She poured each of them more tea. "Prayer and caffeine, in that order."

Something thudded. Screeched. Muttered. (That would be Uncle Miltie.) Metal collided with metal.

Beneath the table, Gracie's beloved, feisty cat Gooseberry snoozed, oblivious to the racket.

"When did Uncle Miltie take up . . . this new hobby?" Marge kept her eye on the ceiling.

"After he saw a special on TV. *Antiquities in Your Attic.*"

"Makes a strong case for V-chips," Marge said, then giggled.

Gracie smiled, too, at the idea of monitoring Uncle Miltie's television watching. Or anything, actually. His stubborn independence was an important part of his personality. He and his wife Doris had loved Gracie like an extra set of doting parents—and had embraced her husband Elmo just as warmly, grieving at his sudden death. Then, when Aunt Doris died two years later, there had been no question in Gracie's mind about inviting Uncle Miltie to come to live with her and Gooseberry. Now, she couldn't imagine life in Willow Bend, Indiana, without him.

Marge sipped tea. "We *will* make enough money, Gracie?

From the auction, I mean. For Patsy's surgery? Then she'll be able to make the trip, won't she?"

Gracie settled onto a stool. "We're not going until spring. She'll have plenty of time to heal before that."

It had been Gracie's idea that Eternal Hope Community Church schedule a bus tour to Eureka Springs for the Passion Play. She'd longed to return ever since she, Elmo and their son Arlen—then a teenager—had stood silent, hands linked, near the Christ of the Ozarks. Now she would finally experience the Passion enacted in that magnificent mountain setting. And having dear friends about her would make it all the sweeter.

No one had been more excited at the prospect of the journey than Patsy Clayton, an adorable but sorely tested child, whose short life had been plagued by far too many medical procedures.

If only this surgery might be the final answer to their prayers, ending Patsy's struggle. *But You know best, Lord. She's such an inspiration to all of us. If braces and walkers are Your plan for her life, help us to accept it. Patsy herself certainly has!*

Uncle Miltie's "Gotcha!" could be heard from afar, and the kitchen ceiling shook under a distant avalanche. Gooseberry jerked awake.

Please. Gracie's eyes squeezed tight. *Please let him be in one piece. And it would be nice, too, if the bedroom survived.*

Wincing with every thud, she traced his slow, bumping

progress from attic to landing . . . to second floor . . . another landing . . . until—

"Look what I found!" Since his voice sounded triumphant, Gracie felt safe opening her eyes. There stood her uncle, all limbs apparently intact.

Marge stage-whispered, "Then there's no need for the fire department?"

"I heard that!" But he was grinning. "You two lovely damsels are invited to view what George Morgan, archeologist extraordinaire, has unearthed!"

Gracie and Marge exchanged raised-eyebrow glances. They rarely called him by his given name, instead using the nickname he'd earned with his ultra-corny jokes, reminiscent of those told long ago by Milton Berle, early television star.

"You'll never guess, Gracie!" His eyes sparkled.

"It's her attic. . . ." Marge reminded him. "She ought to know what's up there."

"Maybe. Maybe not. I was after something Elmo showed me one day. Something his great-great-great somebody carved from wormy chestnut." Carefully, he turned to retrieve whatever treasure his search had yielded.

He held up a carved eagle, nearly life-sized, its unfurling wings swathed in cobwebs. Something deep in Gracie's memory stirred, taking her back to a bright October day when she and El were newly married. There had been foliage so brilliant it seemed incandescent. Elmo perched on a kitchen stool, his newspaper unopened on a windowsill. He'd been watching her bake raised doughnuts when suddenly he said, "We really don't know one another."

She blushed. She was still too new at marriage not to.

"I mean . . . where we've come from. Not our own past, but what went before." He paused. "*Who* went before." Suddenly, he stood and caught her floury hand. "Come with me, Gracie! I want you to meet my ancestors!"

"You don't have them buried in the basement, do you?"

He hugged her tightly, flour and all.

"In the attic," he said, and scarcely gave her time to turn off the heat beneath the heavy iron skillet, half-filled with bubbling shortening. "All those trunks and old crates I stored up there."

And for the next half-hour he had shown her—among other things—the eagle.

The chestnut tree from which it had been carved had stood near the log cabin erected on the Pennsylvania land grant given to one of Elmo's forebears—a Revolutionary War soldier. Later, the tree had loomed over the cabin's spacious brick replacement—only to be shattered by Civil War cannonballs.

"Are you there, Gracie?" Marge waved a bejeweled hand before her friend's glazed eyes.

Gracie forced her wandering attention to the discussion at hand. "Sorry, I was reliving history. Thirty or so pounds ago, when my hair was red without a box of smelly chemicals."

"Before refrigeration?" Marge supplied. "Or even indoor plumbing?"

Gracie smiled. "My memory must not recede as far as *yours*."

Marge winced. *"Touché!"*

"Here's what I want to know, Gracie." Uncle Miltie cleared the tension from his throat. "Would Elmo mind if we contributed it to the auction?"

Gracie felt tears gather in her eyes. "Elmo," she said firmly, "would be delighted." She handed her dear uncle a spray can of lemon-scented furniture polish, and watched as he slowly—almost reverently—released the carving from its attic grime.

"It's...lovely!" Marge exclaimed. "It will be the hit of the auction."

Meanwhile Gooseberry, circling the carving, assessed its every angle. Gracie and Marge followed his example.

It truly was remarkable, Gracie thought, carved so intricately and so long ago. The eagle seemed almost alive, poised for flight, yet its wing and tail feathers were merely suggested by simple, deft slashes. The ruffs around its neck and thighs seemed inflated by wind; its total weight rested on talons grasping a base of original trunk, its bark undisturbed. And the carving's random peppering of unexpected wormholes gave it that irregular texture unique to wormy chestnut.

While Gracie had always been awed by a sculptor's ability to bring wood or metal to life, the history here, linked to El's family, made it even more special.

Marge peered more closely. "Is it my imagination, or is one wing a bit clipped?"

Uncle Miltie glowered. Then he himself indicated some splinters jutting from the beak. "He could've rubbed it a little smoother here."

"It's primitive," Marge pointed out. "The roughness is a part of its charm."

"Maybe," Uncle Miltie replied crisply. "Maybe not."

Marge asked, "Will you varnish it? Or use shellac?"

Uncle Miltie barked in ascending tones, "Varnish? *Shellac?*"

Gracie bent to gather up Gooseberry. She wondered, sometimes, which of them supported the other more in times of need. His purr was a motor that throbbed through his muscles, and his love a perpetual furry comfort. Now he seemed content to cuddle into the curve of her arms, his breath tickling her neck.

"To . . . help protect it?" Marge defended weakly.

Uncle Miltie *hmmphed*.

"I only thought—" Marge was in full retreat.

"Varnish!" Uncle Miltie snarled softly.

Gracie hugged Gooseberry closer.

Suddenly, he struggled from her arms and headed for the screen door—probably in search of Charlotte, Marge's Shih Tzu.

Marge sighed in surrender.

Gracie placed one hand on Marge's, while with the other arm she encircled Uncle Miltie. "You know you both think it's splendid." *I have a career as a buffer zone,* she announced to the Lord—wryly, but comfortably, too.

"Are you truly pleased, Gracie?" Uncle Miltie seemed mollified—perhaps because Marge's mortification seemed complete.

"Absolutely! Your searching for it in that mess of stuff was inspired!"

"Yes. Inspired," Marge echoed flatly. "But how will you protect it?" Marge never could seem to leave bad enough alone.

Uncle Miltie snorted. Grabbing the carving, he stomped out of the room.

"I guess varnish would be a little like pairing a hemp belt with a raw silk ensemble."

Gracie laughed. "Well, at least we're sophisticated enough to describe *objets d'art* that aren't!"

Marge had scarcely left—cradling a pretty pottery dish that held two warm dumplings—when Rocky Gravino arrived, looking for a dose of Gracie's own special brand of good cheer. Nor would he turn down a snack, if offered.

And it would, of course, be offered.

Rocky Gravino, in Gracie's opinion, was the best thing that could have happened to the *Mason County Gazette.* Arriving from Philadelphia to take over the small-town paper as owner and editor, he had made it a much more professionally run operation. He, himself, was an impressive man—not just in his reportorial savvy, but in his uncanny ability to predict when Gracie would be baking.

Just short of the porch steps he paused and inhaled deeply. "Apple," he observed solemnly, "cinnamon pie?"

"Close." Uncle Miltie, seemingly restored to good humor, appeared in time to answer. "Apple dumplings. One each, for Gracie and me. Too bad."

"I know Gracie better than that."

Uncle Miltie eyed him suspiciously. "What brings you here—besides hunger? You hear about our eagle already?"

"Eagle?" Rocky looked interested. "Bald, or golden?"

"Chestnut."

"I never heard—"

"Nor will you," Gracie laughed. "Show him, Uncle Miltie, while I set a meal."

Rocky sighed regretfully. "Just the dumpling, Gracie. I'm on my way from Cordelia's to the office." He grinned sheepishly. "I detoured, actually. I might as well confess."

Uncle Miltie wondered aloud, "I suppose our redoubtable

21

Mrs. Fountain has some new scheme to make her Tourist Home more famous than the White House . . . let me see . . . a flying saucer landed on her roof?"

Rocky chuckled. "Not even close. One of her current guests is a Civil War buff, attracted by all the publicity on that Underground Railroad hiding area. We may have thought there was nothing left to turn up in that old passageway, but it seems he unearthed a journal . . . and, oh yes, a skeleton."

A SKELETON?"

Gracie and Uncle Miltie spoke the word simultaneously.

Rocky cleared his throat. "Fortunately not human." He threw an apologetic glance toward Gooseberry. "Uh—feline," he added softly.

"Was death by . . . natural causes?" Gracie shuddered at the thought of anyone abusing an animal.

"It was buried in a little wooden crate, apparently with great care."

Gracie shook her head sadly.

"Wrapped in a baby blanket," Rocky added. "Obviously someone loved it very much."

Uncle Miltie nibbled a bite of dumpling. "Cordelia will probably pass it off as an ancient Egyptian mummy. They did that with cats, you know."

Gooseberry licked a paw.

Rocky chuckled. "So the Tourist Home probably has a secret tunnel leading somewhere out to the banks of the Nile?"

"Cordelia was never one to let logic get in her way. Or geography." Uncle Miltie winked.

The scene at Eternal Hope Community Church resembled a combination craft show, antique shop, and aftermath of a minor earthquake. Boxes, crates and shopping bags were heaped against the walls.

Some of these, Gracie knew, had come from Pleasant Haven Retirement Home—delivered by Blaise Bloomfield, its activities director, that very afternoon.

At the time, Gracie had been double-checking the inventory of what was on hand so far, making sure that it was all stored in reasonable order. But she hadn't gotten far when a light voice calling her name had broken her concentration. Turning, she'd seen Blaise struggling with an armful of artwork. She was a pretty young woman, sunny and glowing, given to wearing floating skirts that reminded Gracie of summer's butterflies. Gracie guessed she was more than a little romantically interested in Pastor Paul Meyer—there had been many easy-to-read signs—but Eternal Hope's young minister seemed oblivious.

Pausing, Blaise pushed damp tendrils of hair from her forehead. "It looks great, doesn't it? It's bound to be a big success!"

"Fingers crossed! But I think you're right!"

"Want to see what I've brought?"

"Of course."

Carefully, Blaise loosened a layer of protective wrap and heavy cardboard to display an assortment of colorful landscapes and still-life studies, along with a portrait or two of folks Gracie could almost recognize.

Blaise smiled proudly at Gracie. "The residents had a grand old time deciding which of their works might do best at the auction. So many of them know and love Patsy. Did you know she plays word games with some of the wheelchair-bound ladies?"

Gracie was delighted. "Patsy's just a wonderful example to all of us, isn't she?"

Blaise agreed. "She certainly is ... well, I'd better get these things checked in and then head back to work." She glanced around. "It's a lot of work! Are you sure you guys are okay?"

"Why don't you come back and have potluck supper? There'll be more of us then," Gracie said. "And with some pastoral oversight," she emphasized.

"You're a dear." The young woman gave Gracie a quick hug. "And a very wise woman, has anyone told you that?"

"Not yet this afternoon," Gracie laughed.

"Well, I'm here to do it, then. You're not only practically a sage, you're just very, very special. To many people. I know you are to me and to ... Paul." She lowered her voice as she said his name. "Well . . . I'd better be getting back, or they'll hire someone else to referee shuffleboard!" With a quick wave, she hurried the dolly to the corner where Lester Twomley and Linda Cantrell accepted and recorded items for auction.

Now Estelle Livett and Nancyalma Smith arranged home-canned fruits and jewellike jars of preserves that had been donated. Pastor Paul Meyer—whose shepherding skills for-tunately surpassed any knack he had for carpentry—was struggling with a hammer, spikes and two-by-fours, whose intended function escaped Gracie.

He'll be pleased when he sees Blaise at his table, won't he? she found herself asking the Lord for reassurance. *And will we ever be ready by Saturday?* Immediately, she apologized. *How can I doubt, when so many of Your good workers are here? And, where even two or three are gathered in Your name . . . any task is lighter,* she concluded.

She turned in a slow circle, surveying the chaos. It was hard to see the Lord's hand or any lightness in such a mess. *Still,* she continued, more for herself than Him, *You created the world out of worse . . . even if we don't have six days, only two.*

"Have you ever seen such . . . ?" Bert Benton, baritone in the church choir, seemed at a loss for words.

"Wreckage?" Don Delano suggested. He carried a step-ladder, destined, it seemed, for Pastor Paul.

"Potential!" Teenaged Amy Cantrell sang out as she

sailed past, a banner floating behind her. "It's going to be wonderful—isn't it, Gracie?"

Bert Benton paused, resting the ladder. "That young woman is something else. Gives us parents of future teenagers hope."

Gracie wondered if he contrasted Amy's positive nature with his own son's surly disposition. *How is it, Lord, that nice people like the Bentons so often produce rotten kids?* Immediately, she corrected herself. God loved Barry Benton every bit as much as He loved Amy—*although even You must find loving him a stretch.*

A frenzy of hammering brought her back to present problems.

Lord, maybe I'm getting old—why else would a challenge like this fail to energize me? Give her a catering task and she was in her element. Let ingredients cloud the air and pots clutter surfaces, with containers heaped over sink and counters— and she was unconquerable. But this. . .

Choir risers had been dragged out of storage, undoubtedly for use by Rick Harding—who was to be the auctioneer—and his helpers. A small table held gavel, cash boxes, an electric adding machine, various calculators and an array of supplies, including pads, paper clips, a couple of staplers and a rainbow of colored markers.

In the part of the large room closest to the kitchen, Barb Jennings and the Turner twins—Tish and Tyne—were stretching white plastic over the long tables where auction goers would consume Gracie's famous chili, garlic breadsticks and cobbler. Other choir members had promised salads, and Nancyalma Smith, a contralto gifted with more volume than accuracy, was to be responsible for the various fixings to go with the chili.

The Turner twins glanced up and waved, obviously having a good time as they chatted and giggled.

Gracie walked over to join them. Barb laughed with the twins. The pair could have passed for much younger than their thirty-something years—until close examination revealed an occasional silver hair straying from their blond ponytails, and the suggestion of crow's feet at the corners of their Wedgewood blue eyes.

Tish gestured. "Well, Gracie," she began, and Tyne continued, "What do you think?" They were known for completing one another's sentences, as well as for dressing similarly—despite the fact that both were married and maintaining separate households. Today they wore embroidered denim shirts over stone-washed jeans. Both stood, hands on hips, looking expectant.

"Wonderful!" Gracie said. "As always."

Barb, looking tired, pulled up a chair and sank into it. Yet Gracie knew that if anyone mentioned music, this choir's director, talented organist and designated worrier would suddenly find her trademark energy.

Pausing to rub Barb's shoulders gently, Gracie thought, *How I love these people, Lord, and so do You. You've blessed each of us so richly—with the talents of music, cooking, ministry, love, so much more. . . . This event will come together, hard as that seems to imagine now. And with You blessing our efforts, we'll make enough to finance Patsy's surgery. But even if not—*

"Look at these!" A shriek short-circuited Gracie's prayer. Much as she hated putting the Lord on hold, she joined the crowd converging on the choir's only soprano with "professional credentials," as Estelle Livett never failed to remind them.

"Aren't they darling!" Estelle held aloft a sculpture of a rabbit with large, soulful eyes. Except for the limpid brown eyes, it was the nearly translucent white of fine polished marble, with—

"Is that a wick?" Gracie asked, leaning closer.

"Of course not!" Estelle protested, then gasped. "A candle? My goodness! I didn't realize. . ."

"Clever," Barb observed. "Carved from wax! But who would ever want burn it? It's so charming!"

Altogether, there were three candle creatures: the rabbit, a squirrel and a skunk. Each was approximately one-third life-sized, and while there had been no real effort to render them realistic, there was a quirky appeal to their originality. They "suggested" what they depicted in a manner more compelling than if they had been true to life.

Gracie felt instinctively that there was something calming about them. Something unusual. A tranquility. An ... innocence? Maybe that was the word. She knew she'd never seen anything quite like them.

Even Estelle was smiling. "I wonder who the artisan is?" She turned the rabbit sculpture. "N.A.M.S.," she read slowly, frowning. "N.A.M.S.? Who has four initials?"

A croaking voice Gracie could not identify whispered, "I don't know, but they should bring a good price."

Gracie was not the only one to turn. It was Rick Harding.

"Are you trying to scare us?" Marge demanded. "What happened to the tenor tones we all thrill to?"

"Laryngitis," he managed to say faintly. His daughter Lillian wriggled in his arms. "It looks like there's no way I can be an auctioneer Saturday." The effort to speak wore him out, and the little girl slipped happily out of his grasp.

"We'd have planned for a silent auction if you'd given us more advance warning," Gracie joked—but she wasn't smiling.

3

WHAT IN THE WORLD are we going to do?"

The auction committee had met in emergency session. One of the few African Americans in Willow Bend and an all-around good guy, Rick had quickly become someone every choir member—excluding Estelle who resented his music credentials—deferred to. With his beautiful tenor voice and array of skills, he had endeared himself quickly to his fellow singers, and Gracie was far from alone in feeling grateful that his computer company had thought to transfer him to rural Indiana.

"Sometimes," Bert Benton offered, "laryngitis . . . lasts for weeks." Hearing what he'd just said, he groaned.

Tish Ball cleared her throat before beginning shyly, "We could pray. . . ."

"For a miracle!" Tyne Anderson bounced in her chair.

"After all, if miracles don't still happen . . ."

"Why are we here?" The twins nodded to one another in appreciation of their grasp of the situation.

If only dear Elmo were still alive, he would have made the perfect substitute auctioneer. "I miss you," Gracie thought.

"Who else is there?" Amy Cantrell asked. "There has to be someone."

"Does it have to be a man?" Estelle asked.

"Yes!" came a chorus of voices as one. Not because they were sexist—not at all, Gracie was sure—but because Estelle was so obviously angling to nominate herself.

Poor Estelle, Gracie confided to the Lord. *She has a tin ear for human relations, doesn't she?* She paused, considering. She knew God accepted Estelle even when her fellow choir members were dubious.

"Who? Who? Who?" Barb asked, tapping her chin with each utterance. Amy hid a giggle behind her hand. If she kept it up, Barb would sound more like a contemplative owl than a hardworking choir director.

"I . . . have an idea." Nancyalma Smith raised a tentative hand.

When she went no further, Estelle quickly showed her exasperation. "Not you, I hope! Come on, Nance. Spit it out!"

"My . . . brother."

Silence followed a few initial gasps.

"Your brother?" Amy said brightly. "Oh, Mrs. Smith, I didn't know you had one!"

"He's . . . visiting."

In all the years since she'd come to Willow Bend as Elmo's bride, Gracie had seen Montgomery X. Montgomery only a few times. Each time he had "visited" his sister, it was only because he was down and out, needing a place to stay until he could cook up some new moneymaking scheme. Elmo, who had perhaps been opinionated but never judgmental, had quipped once that Monty gave the term "ne'er-do-well" new dimension.

The group was silent. Gracie felt it would be only courteous to ask when Monty had arrived in town.

"Thanks, Gracie." Nancyalma's voice shook, just a bit. "Montgomery arrived just last night. Rather late. And I presume you were going to ask next whether he's ever had any experience as an auctioneer." She squared her shoulders. "And the answer is—yes!"

"I guess I never met him." Uncle Miltie seemed more interested in his hot fudge sundae than in Marge's near-hysteria.

"*Hmmph!*" Marge waved her dessert spoon for emphasis, spattering ice cream that Gooseberry volunteered to clean up. "He might be a wonderful auctioneer. I wouldn't know. But I do know that Montgomery X. Montgomery can't be trusted around money. Not for a minute." She leaned forward and said in a stage whisper, "And he'll be right there, where it's all collected. The bank will be closed until Monday morning, and there's more security in my freezer compartment than there is in the church safe! Which means—"

"Cool cash," Uncle Miltie told her, quite pleased with himself. "Frozen assets. Which reminds me. Ever hear what the friendly watch dog said when his owner threatened to take him to the pound?"

Marge rolled her eyes.

Uncle Miltie waited.

"All right, go ahead. You will, anyway." Marge rested her dripping spoon on the edge of her dish, and Gooseberry meowed his disapproval. "I said, go ahead, I'll bite."

"Exactly," Uncle Miltie seemed relieved his straight woman had come through.

"Exactly what?"

"That's what he said. The dog," he hastened to explain. "When his owner threatened to send him to the pound, he said, 'All right. I'll bite.'"

Gracie and Marge couldn't help but laugh. Uncle Miltie was incorrigible—always had been, always would be.

"And then, of course, since you mentioned refrigerators—"

"Another one?" Marge looked resigned.

"Be glad to," Uncle Miltie paid no attention.

Gracie had to smile. Uncle Miltie liked nothing better than to drive Marge to distraction, which he did so well. And so often.

"What did the salad dressing say when it was offered a job?"

Marge just sighed.

Uncle Miltie took another bite of ice cream.

"I don't know," Marge grumbled.

"Why would it say that?"

Marge's temper was teetering.

"Uncle Miltie," Gracie suggested mildly.

He nodded. "The salad dressing had applied for a job—"

"What kind of salad dressing?" Marge snapped.

"Take your pick."

"Thousand Island."

"Thousand Island it is."

"What kind of job?"

Uncle Miltie was agreeable, still. "Any kind of job you want!" He waited patiently to pounce.

"Bus driver, then." Marge swirled her spoon in the melting dessert.

"How is salad dressing going to drive a bus?"

Marge shrugged. "As easily as it could apply for any job, I guess."

Gracie grinned. Once in a while, her uncle deserved a dose of his own medicine. "Comeuppance," her grandmother would have called it.

"Woman," Uncle Miltie fumed as he pushed to his feet, "you kill a joke faster than anyone I know!"

"Some jokes deserve a merciless death."

Marge then relented. "Come on," she coaxed, "what did

the Thousand Island salad dressing say when it was offered a job? Driving a bus?" she couldn't seem to resist adding with a grin.

"I have a perfect mind not to tell you!"

"Gracie will bake a batch of snickerdoodles tomorrow if you do."

He looked to Gracie, and she nodded.

"Okay then. It said, 'Lettuce discuss celery.' Get it?" And he stomped off, his reputation intact.

Montgomery X. Montgomery, whatever else might be said of him, proved to be an efficient, effective auctioneer. He certainly had the patter down: "Five, five, I have five. Ten—ten—ten—ten. Come on, folks, you're missing the trolley here! Ten, ten, I have seven-fifty—now eight, now nine, and—a ten, ten, ten . . . I got ten, fifteen—"

He also looked the part—striped open-necked shirt, long sleeves turned up. An unlit cigar protruded from the inside pocket of his checked vest. A too-small, narrow-brimmed hat with a wide rust-colored satin band sat well back on his head. His oversized wristwatch, rimless glasses and coppery hair (long in back, sparse in front) all reflected the overhead light. Beads of sweat glistened as he determinedly auctioned one item after another. Jabbing his stubby forefinger at reluctant bidders, practically prancing in front of the assembled

Willow Bend townsfolk, he consistently achieved a price higher than reason suggested.

"He's a wizard!" Gracie ladled chili as she kept track of the auction's progress.

"Con artist, more like it." Marge knew one when she met one, and would be the first to say she'd had her troubles with fast-talking, unreliable men.

"But a very good con artist," Gracie said.

"If there *is* such a thing." Marge was adamant.

"Well, everyone deserves a second chance," Gracie protested mildly.

"I'd sooner sit down and let your uncle tell me awful jokes for an hour than I'd give Monty Montgomery credit for anything."

"Going ... going ... gone!" came the voice of Nancyalma's miscreant brother. And *bang!* went his gavel. "Sold!"

4

AS THE RISING AND FALLING RHYTHMS of the auction continued, and as the lunch crowd swelled, then abated, Gracie found herself seeking the Lord's ear.

It seems we might even exceed our goal, doesn't it, Lord? You do use the most unlikely among us, don't You—to work Your will? Who could have guessed that Rick's laryngitis might turn out to be a good thing—not for him, of course—but You and I both know that Rick could never have wheedled such exorbitant sums—and made people enjoy being robbed.

And what about this Montgomery X. Montgomery, Lord? Is Willow Bend a part of Your plan for him? Is there something he's to learn here? Something we're to teach him? And is Marge right? Do we really have to watch him around the money? There are certainly plenty of us to keep an eye on him, and he's got very little space to maneuver in, if malfeasance is on his mind.

She wanted—even needed—to ask Him more, but a new group of folks eager for their bowls of chili required her full attention.

Patsy Clayton, her mini-walker neatly folded and leaned against the end of the table, took the tiniest possible bites of Gracie's peach cobbler.

"I'm just too nervous to eat, Mrs. Parks," she said, "like in Vacation Bible School when we had crafts and treats at the same time, and had to figure out how to eat the brownies but not the glitter on our fingers.

"I really like crafts, don't you? There's just something really exciting about seeing things people make, like the eagle carved by that ancestor of your husband's, how it looks as though it's just about ready to fly."

Patsy took another nibble. "And this is soooo good! Well, if I eat slowly."

"Thank you, Patsy." Gracie turned away to hide a smile. *This child is an inspiration to all of us, Lord,* she thought. *Crippled since birth, and all those surgeries, with little more to look forward to, it seemed, than another operation. If You were here, You could touch those poor little legs and tell her to take that walker to recycling. Then she could leap like the lame man You healed—and go out to run, jump and play with the other children. But You must have something different—even better—in mind for our beloved Patsy. . . .*

She was such a bright, eager child in Bible School—asking

the questions that required deep answers. Her mind turned up thoughtful responses that often to Gracie seemed fresh and original, though never disrespectful.

"Isn't that the ugliest thing you ever saw?" Patsy asked in a whisper, one hand cupping her mouth.

Currently up for bids was a hooked throw rug belonging to Estelle, who had boasted of its eye-catching modernist design. Personally, Gracie found Patsy's critical assessment more accurate.

"Just look at this, folks," Monty announced, with an exaggerated tone of admiration. "You don't want to miss the steamboat on this one-of-a-kind example of hand-crafted artistry! This elegant tapestry is fashioned from the finest alpaca yarns dyed with natural herbal tints in jewel-like tones. It's going to be a lucky person who takes this beauty home! So, what do I hear, ladies and gents? An opening bid of—let's say conservatively, three hundred, three hundred, I want three hundred, give me three hundred . . . three hundred . . . three hundred—"

He wiped his forehead with a large red handkerchief. "I can see you're going to make me work on this one! But don't be bashful, folks. This is an heirloom your relatives will fight to possess. It's a museum piece, for sure, you can take it from me. But since you insist on being conservative, let me hear two hundred, two hundred, two hundred—" He reached for a glass of water. "Think of it, folks. . . ." He paused, clearing his throat. "You're making me hoarse, here."

Laughter rippled, but no bids were forthcoming.

"Let me put it this way." He looked out at the crowd, an earnest expression on his face. "Just close your eyes. That's right. It's a cold winter night . . . wind howling like demented banshees, cold sneaking through cracks you never knew were there . . . and all you want to do is escape to some sunny spot. And there's that rug . . . your rug, bought here today. You reach down, place it on your knee, and it's like some magic carpet sweeping you—" He paused to listen to the hooting and whistling rushing up at him. "Please," he begged. "Give me a bid, any bid."

"Ten dollars," someone offered.

Embarrassed for Estelle, Gracie raised her hand. "Fifty." She wondered what she'd do with the thing—certainly not ask Gooseberry to sleep on it. She valued his good taste too much for that.

"Thank you, madam," Montgomery said with feeling. "I now have fifty, fifty, fifty, could I have fifty-one? Fifty-one? Anyone? No one? Going . . . going . . . gone, to this wise pur-chaser with the russet locks."

With everyone watching, Gracie tried to look like the pleased and proud new owner of a desirable item. She could see Estelle out of the corner of her eye and knew she was shamelessly soliciting further admiration for her former possession. It was all Gracie's now: an acquisition that fell squarely into the no-good-deed-goes-unpunished category.

As a helper delivered Gracie's rug, Patsy finished her cobbler and handed her bowl to Gracie just as Elmo's eagle went up for bids.

"Oh! I want to see!" Patsy pushed from the table, grabbed her walker, and moved slowly away to stand by Uncle Miltie's elbow.

Gracie lifted a little prayer. When she raised her glance, it was to see Pastor Paul and Blaise strolling toward her. Blaise, wearing a white t-shirt under a daisy-yellow jumper, looked like a woman with a happy secret. At the moment, Paul was bent toward her, talking animatedly, his hands emphasizing each phrase. His companion, glancing upward, seemed to glow.

Is he blind, Lord? Gracie wondered.

"Gracie!" Pastor Paul's grin widened. "We've been discussing a new program here at Eternal Hope, hoping to involve more of the folks from Peaceful Haven."

"He's been discussing." Blaise plunked herself down. "I've been listening! But then—

"We decided we needed food," Pastor Paul filled in. "Brain food."

"What can I get you?" Gracie asked. "The chili can be spicy or not, as you prefer."

"We'll each have a spicy bowl, right, Blaise?" He offered that boyish grin that would melt the heart of a glacier. His companion nodded, almost dreamily, it seemed to Gracie. The young woman would probably be wise not to be so open in her infatuation, Gracie decided, but then realized it hardly mattered since Pastor Paul obviously wasn't catching any signals, anyway.

Blaise waited for Paul to decide between the chopped scallions and sour cream toppings and the shredded cheddar and chopped avocado. She and Gracie both smiled when they saw him take a little of each chili "extra."

"Have you had Gracie's legendary garlic breadsticks?" he asked Blaise.

Blaise accepted one, along with an extra pat of butter.

"Some of our residents complain the chili they serve at the home is too bland. But this build-it-yourself way is the answer!" Her own dish was daintily piled with fresh tomato salsa.

"Gracie," Paul said. "Willow Bend eats extravagantly well . . . and has you to thank for it." Blaise Bloomfield nodded her agreement.

As they strolled off, Gracie sneaked a spoonful of her own famous chili.

"Whew!" Uncle Miltie blew across a steaming cup of coffee. In the background, Monty Montgomery encouraged spirited bidding for the unusual animal sculptures. "I thought sure that woman would get it."

That woman: Marge.

Marge, wanting the eagle for her shop window, had been willing to bid vigorously. Only when the price reached dizzying heights had she dropped out.

"It was great to see it climb so high. It was almost as if El was personally helping out Patsy."

"Should buy her a decent portion of operating room time."

"All the way from incision to stitches, I'd guess."

He sipped his coffee. "The medical costs these days! You practically have to rent a Band-Aid!"

"Mr. Morgan?"

Uncle Miltie turned.

Even if she hadn't often seen his photo in the various newspapers—as well as on re-election posters—Gracie would have thought the tall man looked like a politician. It wasn't just the pin-striped suit and star-spangled tie, when nearly everyone else was dressed casually. Nor was it the booming voice, wide smile, or hearty back-slap that almost toppled Uncle Miltie from his perch. It was the eyes.

Not that I have anything against politicians, Lord, she assured Him, *not when they're sincere. Not when they're public servants in the truest sense. Not when they can look You straight in the eye.*

But this man's glance darted everywhere, never quite settling on anyone or anything.

Her uncle seemed to share her assessment. He waited stiffly.

"Tyrone Sanders," the man said, thrusting his hand forward.

Acting as if he didn't see it, Uncle Miltie took a bite of cobbler. "Don't know whether I prefer your peach or your cherry, my dear."

Tyrone Sanders cleared his throat. "Is there any cobbler left?" he asked.

Gracie was trying to decide how to reply—after all, the Lord sent strangers to test us and no one should be judged—when Sanders chuckled. "I'm somewhat of a connoisseur," he boomed. "Just want to see if my friend here knows his cobblers the way he claims to."

Uncle Miltie sniffed, "I not only know my cobbler, I know I don't know you."

Gracie watched the two of them anxiously.

"Well," Sanders said, his voice dropping to a confidential tone, "you sure do know your carved eagles. That's a real prize I bought today."

Uncle Miltie, though still wary, took a posture that was a little less hostile.

"Your eagle, sir—" Sanders paused, obviously to increase the dramatic effect of what he was about to say. "Your eagle will rest on a marble pedestal at the foot of the magnificent stairway in Mason County Courthouse!"

It's all Uncle Miltie can do, Lord, she confided in her

thoughts, *not to show pleasure. You gave him more than his share of stubbornness, that's for certain.*

"Not really mine, though," her uncle told Sanders, pointing toward Gracie with a forkful of cobbler. "It belonged to my niece, Gracie."

"Yours, Gracie?"

"Mrs. Parks to you," Uncle Miltie corrected. "Mrs. Elmo Parks. The eagle was her late husband's."

Gracie was starting to feel a bit sorry for Sanders until he reached for her hand and said softly, "Elmo was a lucky man, Gracie, you're a very handsome woman and a splendid cook, to boot." Unable to pull her hand away, she allowed him to pat it once or twice.

Uncle Miltie's face reddened.

"I intend that there be a plaque, recognizing the source of the eagle. And my question for you, sir, at this time is, Do you want to do the repairs, or should we?"

Uncle Miltie frowned. "Repairs?"

"Yes. Sanding. Filling in those wormholes. Painting. The carving's finish needs . . ."

Uncle Miltie stood up with more energy than grace. Where had he left his walker? Gracie wondered. And where was all this leading? Into trouble, was her quick conclusion.

"P-p-p—" he sputtered, and Gracie had to hide a smile, remembering his reaction when Marge had suggested varnish.

"You'd actually p-paint a priceless antique?"

"Not priceless, precisely." Sanders leaned back with a smug smile. "I bought it, you'll remember."

"We want it back!"

"I'm afraid—"

"Don't we, Gracie?"

"Oh, Uncle Miltie, I think—"

"Your niece here knows you can't back out now! It was a legitimate sale—"

"I beg to differ!" Uncle Miltie thundered. "I don't call it legitimate if you plan to violate it with spray enamel!"

"I assure you—"

"Red, white and blue, I suppose. With stars pasted over the eyes!"

"Mr. Morgan—Mrs. Parks—it would be tastefully done, I assure you!"

"And I assure you—" With each word Uncle Miltie's finger came nearer to Sanders's chest. "—that eagle would better have been left in our attic than polluted with paint and planted in some rundown courthouse where stuffed-shirts like you—" He had run out of steam.

Gracie willed her voice to calmness. "Mr. Sanders," she said equably, "the eagle obviously had great sentimental value for my husband. It was carved by one of his forebears. Paint would diminish not only the honor of its being displayed but also the actual worth of the eagle itself. Mr. Morgan and I would be happy to reimburse you—"

"Better than that!" A voice broke in.

Startled, Gracie and Uncle Miltie both turned.

"I'll give you double what you paid," Marge continued confidently. She bestowed an extra wide smile on Tyrone Sanders, whose jaw had dropped. "And I promise you, Uncle Miltie, I won't paint or varnish it! I won't even dust it, without your permission."

5

WHILE NANCYALMA, Barb Jennings and the Turner twins huddled over heaps of stacked bills and checks, their adding machines clacking in counterpoint, Marge and Gracie finished wiping down the kitchen and dining area. As quickly as a table could be cleared, Les Twomley and his crew unlocked and folded the legs. Already, most of the chairs had been stored away.

"Notice our esteemed auctioneer?" Marge spoke in a stage whisper. Uncle Miltie and Patsy Clayton, who was waiting for her mother to return, looked up.

Montgomery X. Montgomery hovered behind his sister. His gaze never seemed to leave the stack of auction receipts. A charitable interpretation would be he was simply admiring the results of his own effort.

Oh, Lord . . . Gracie began, then didn't know how to continue. But God was familiar enough with the symptoms of human avarice to know what she feared. The Scriptures were littered with evidence of greed. Even if Judas Iscariot's motives were only to hasten Christ's Kingdom, there were always Ananias and Sapphira. And Laban and his sons— begrudging Jacob his hard-earned wealth. Lot, in his dealings with his uncle Abraham. Nabal, dismissing the needs of David and his band. . . . *There's no end, is there, Lord, to our wanting and reaching for more?* She felt a tightening in her heart. *But this*—this *money is for Patsy's surgery. If only we'd buy another safe, or a new lock for the old one—somehow, we never get around to it. Lord, You know we have other priorities.*

She'd bring it up at the next board meeting, she decided— not for the first time. But that would be far too late for this present emergency. Still, how could Monty ever have the nerve to abscond with their money or pull any kind of shenanigan with so many people already mistrusting his character?

Without looking directly at Marge, Uncle Miltie began, "Maybe Marge's shop would be a good place to stick the dough. Aren't you going back there now?"

"Yes, I do have to relieve the nice young woman—Vivian Traub—who's minding it for me. But I don't have any better safe than the church's. A lot of my business is credit card sales and I put my cash deposit in the bank drop."

"Well, I forgot about the night deposit, but we don't have a proper account or any deposit slips." Uncle Miltie sighed. "How about we just ask them to open up?"

"The locks are set not to open until Monday morning."

Marge suggested, "We could each offer to keep some of it until then—divide it up. That way there wouldn't be so much—" Her glance flicked toward Montgomery X. Montgomery, who was blithely bagging coins.

Uncle Miltie watched him for a moment before replying, "Not a bad idea. I guess."

Gracie wasn't certain. How would Nancyalma react if they suggested such a thing? They never had worried about the proceeds after a rummage sale, or a Saturday night ham loaf dinner. At Eternal Hope, trust was their most abundant currency.

"If we're going to do it—" Beckoning for Marge and Gracie to follow him, Uncle Miltie walked toward the counting table.

"We were just thinking" Uncle Miltie began, but Nancyalma's delighted crow interrupted him.

"Gracie! Marge! Everyone! Did you ever see such a haul?"

Unfortunate word, Gracie thought—often associated with such terms as *heist* or *loot*, for example.

"We've never had such a successful day! Patsy's surgery is secure, if this is any indication!

"And be assured," she said, her eyes earnest, "I'll lock the house very, very carefully these two nights . . . and hide the money so even a bloodhound couldn't unearth it." She laughed. "Why, I have hiding places even I haven't discovered!"

Gracie knew that to be true. Nancyalma's house was, in

fact, a challenge to the unwary. Plants stood everywhere. "My tropical rain forest," Nancyalma liked to say, "right here in Indiana."

The lushness of the foliage was truly startling. One split-leaf philodendron of amazing circumference pressed gigantic leaves against the ceiling. A palm with wide fan-shaped leaves shouldered into the platform rocker, and a vining philodendron circumnavigated two adjoining rooms, its roots anchored in a ceramic pot on the mantel and its various tendrils supported by paste-up hooks and twisties.

But it was not only nature that crowded the small home. There must be something about a plant jungle that encouraged further clutter.

Bookshelves lining the walls overflowed into heaps stacked around the floor, and no flat surface was left bare of antique bottles and ceramic figurines. There were several generations of mementos, photos in dusty frames, and a welter of unopened junk mail and unanswered letters.

"Every once in a while there's an avalanche," Nancyalma was fond of saying, "or I go on an archaeological dig—and while I often can't find what I'm looking for, other treasures surface. It's kind of fun, really, if you don't mind living in an uncatalogued museum. Think Aladdin's cave!"

Nancyalma huffed and puffed through life with just that sort of cheerful acceptance. Her pleasant plumpness was the kind that made Gracie think of storybook grandmas offering graham crackers for dunking in milk. Her hair, once a nondescript mouse-color, now sparkled with silver along its deep waves. Her round face nearly always crinkled into a smile that formed cavernous dimples. Except for Sundays and funerals, she was rarely without a bibbed apron with two large pockets.

At the moment, those pockets bulged with slips of paper. She added pencils and pens as she gathered the accumulated money into a large canvas tote. *Souvenir of Plymouth Rock*, it read.

"Never fear," she assured them. "The money will get to the bank Monday morning, nine o'clock sharp."

That's what we're afraid of, Lord, Gracie thought. *But You are able . . . in all things . . . and You know all hearts. Forgive me for judging. Amen.*

ॐ

"So the auction yesterday was a huge success." Abe Wasserman set a frosted pitcher of iced tea in the center of the table, and sat down for their Sunday lunchtime chat. "It is a marvelous thing," he said softly, "to help a child. The blessing that remains far exceeds the blessing given."

"As with all love," Gracie suggested, pouring Rocky a glass of tea. She had met them there, as usual, after services.

"Perhaps not all."

Pitcher poised, Gracie waited. *I feel a story coming,* she

confided to the Lord, *and I am always enriched by Abe's stories. How thoughtful of You to bring such wisdom to tiny Willow Bend, where we could so easily fall into a narrow way of seeing life.*

"There was a certain king," Abe began, "of a certain pagan land noted for its richness of natural beauty and mineral wealth. King—we shall call him Herman for want of a loftier name—was much loved for his generous spirit. Whenever his palace was visited by foreign dignitaries, and rich foods were prepared for banquets in their honor, King Herman was careful to invite the poor of the valleys and villages, that they too might enjoy the celebration. In particular, he loved having the children nearby.

"His oldest son and heir, however, resented sharing his father's bounties with grubby children, with poor villagers, and even with foreign heads of state. 'When I am king,' young Pompus muttered, 'things will be different.' And they were. With King Herman scarcely buried, young, recently crowned King Pompus hired builders to erect a huge wall so that the palace could not be viewed from the valleys and villages. There were no gates, and only one narrow window where deliveries could be passed. On those rare occasions when an errand must be run, a skinny servant had to squeeze through that cramped aperture.

"Now servants polished the golden dishes for Pompus's use alone. The king ordered the foods he preferred in quantities so small that nothing was left for anyone else, even the palace dogs. 'Why should I share?' he asked himself. 'Only I am worthy of such wealth.'"

Abe paused to take a contemplative sip of tea. Impatient for Abe to continue, Rocky rattled the shrinking ice cubes in his glass. Even when hearing a fable, he had a newsman's need to get all the facts as quickly as possible.

"Eventually," Abe continued, "young King Pompus even began to resent the fact that his servants needed to handle his possessions—serving and polishing his golden platters, dusting his gleaming furniture, whisking and hanging the royal robes. 'Enough of this!' he stormed one particular day. 'Out! Out, all of you, I say! You are dismissed from any service here! And be certain you steal nothing that is mine—not so much as a dead leaf off the trees!'"

Gracie hadn't heard Amy Cantrell come over to take their order. Looking up to smile at her, she realized everyone seated nearby in the deli was hushed and listening.

Amy had brought them a basket of miniature Danish pastries. The carefully filled treats—apricot, blueberry and her special cheese—could mean only one person: Sophie.

Sophie Glass, Abe's sister, divided her time among three sites: her apartment in Cleveland; the "Promised Land" of Florida—where she longed to have Abe join her; and her brother's Willow Bend deli. Nothing pleased her more than receiving compliments from Abe's customers for her personally baked delicacies.

"All day every day, and far into every night," Abe was continuing, "King Pompus rejoiced in his aloneness and gloated over his treasures. But there came a time when even they were not enough . . . when he coveted ownership of the mountains glinting silver in the moonlight. He yearned to own the moon. He grieved that the blue summer sky belonged as completely to the villagers as to him—and however he tried, he could not contain the birds and their music within his walls alone."

Everyone watched Abe expectantly. He smiled benevolently, waiting a beat or two. "There is no blessing in the love of self."

For a moment, all was silent.

Rocky chuckled appreciatively. "You never fail to have a story—always an appropriate one. However, my wise friend, I do have one small question—concerning logistics."

"I shall certainly answer—as I am able." Abe winked in Gracie's direction.

"How is it—with only that small space for exit or entrance—a space so small, you'll remember, that only a very slim servant could squeeze through—how then, did all of the servants leave when he dismissed them? Surely not all could fit through the eye of that particular needle!" He leaned back, a contented expression playing around his lips.

Gracie shook her head. This was a game both men enjoyed. It was her job to listen, jumping in only as needed.

"You know, you're right," Abe admitted. "I believe there

was a cook named Esmeralda—who never prepared a dish she didn't sample first—amply." He nodded. "And the blacksmith, of course. Rufus. His shoulders were as wide as an ox-beam."

"Then ..." prompted Rocky.

"Ah, yes! How did they get out? A difficult question indeed, since Pompus strictly prohibited any breaching of the wall." To Gracie he confided, "That would have meant using tools that belonged to Pompus."

"*Sooooooo?*" Rocky spread his upturned hands. "How—"

Abe looked beyond Rocky's shoulder and smiled. "Ah, saved by sweet Amy!"

The teenager stood with her pen poised over her order pad. "I didn't want to interrupt until you were finished. Besides, it's one of my favorites! There are ones I just love hearing over and over, and each time they're a little different."

"He isn't finished yet," Rocky said, agreeably, "though I guess you've helped buy him some time to think of an answer."

Abe chortled. "I may have to postpone my answer until I've consulted my ... reference ... books again. But simply to forestall hunger, my clever friend, I believe a tunnel was involved ... or perhaps a hot air balloon."

Amy spoke with admiration. "Gosh, Mr. Gravino! I never thought of that when I heard the story!"

Abe interjected quickly, "Take their orders, young lady."

Gracie leaned back contentedly, going over in her mind the many levels of Abe's parable. Sometimes his deli was practically a ministry, or at least a pulpit. But, then, as she knew from her own experience, feeding bodies was often as important as feeding souls. The grand thing was that Abe did both.

"Yes, sir." Amy straightened, suddenly professional. "What would you like today? Your usuals?"

It wasn't until she had turned away that Gracie noticed her limp. "Amy, dear!" she called. "Were you limping this morning in choir?"

Amy grimaced. "Can you imagine anybody so clumsy? I turned my ankle—walking home." Resting her hand on a table, she surveyed the Ace bandage. "But the funniest thing, Gracie. You know those amazing wax carvings at the auction yesterday? The animals?"

Gracie nodded.

"Well, when I got to work after church, someone had left me one. A turtle. Really cute. I wonder who—"

Abe broke in. "An admirer who'd rather be anonymous. Romance is best when there's anticipation. Someone's softening you up!"

Amy's sweet expression was replaced by a frown. "I don't think so. You'd tell me if it was one of you?" When they nodded, she sighed. "I was sort of hoping it would be. One of you, that is. I guess mysteries just make me a little bit . . . uncomfortable."

6

SOPHIE APPEARED from the kitchen just as they were finishing the last bites of lunch. They complimented her on the tiny perfect Danish pastries.

"I put up those peaches myself." Sophie boasted. "They're rare-ripes. They all but fell from the tree to meet me. It was warm, a very warm day even for so early in September. A few of the maple leaves had just begun to turn, but the birds hadn't felt the call south yet—nor had I." She laughed.

"I keep telling her," Abe said fondly, "that she should write a cookbook."

Sophie replied, "If anyone here should write a cookbook—it's you, Gracie Lynn Parks!"

"We could do one together. Ecumenical eating! Interfaith entertaining!" Gracie waved her arm to indicate the deli's many happy patrons.

"Everyone's stomach works the same," Abe said philosophically.

"Especially when there's been too much food put in them!" Rocky groaned, holding his abdomen in mock distress.

As they laughed together, pleasure flooded Gracie's awareness of the moment. Her fondness and gratitude to these dear people was incalculable. *To You, Lord. You have given us so much . . . and so many . . . to love. The friendships You provide are exactly the ones we need.*

"Sorry to break this up." Rocky scraped back his chair. "But I'm expecting a call from overseas. It's not today there. . . ." He ran his fingers through his thick salt-and-pepper hair. "But I'm not certain whether it's yesterday or tomorrow."

Sophie said, "Well, I know all about springing back and falling forward . . . or is it the other way around?"

Again they laughed. Rocky caught Gracie's hands in his and said, "See you later, dear girl." Then he included all of them in a wide wave. "So long, friends."

It was high time, Gracie decided, that she stop by Cordelia Fountain's. With the rush of preparation for the auction—and then the day itself—she'd had neither time nor energy for a social call.

She did have to admit, though, that she was curious about Cordelia's new historical find. The tourist home owner's obsessive interest in local history could sometimes become a bit wearing, but she was right in that it made Willow Bend more interesting to visitors.

When the mood seized her, Cordelia greeted visitors to her popular tourist home dressed in period costume, sunbonnet and all. The only thing spoiling the picture, however, was that she preferred to wear running shoes. How many times had Gracie heard her say, "Even a Southern belle isn't the best company if her feet hurt"? And Gracie answered her as she always did. "That would be southern Indiana. Maybe Illinois?"

Cordelia now patted a space next to her on the front-porch swing. "I've wondered why you haven't been over."

Gracie sank gratefully into the soft cushion. "My, this feels good! And it isn't as though I haven't been sitting most of today! Sunday School and church, then lunch at Abe's."

Cordelia made a wry face. "That awful 1950s décor of his—not a very aesthetically pleasing period! I keep suggesting to him that he redo it, to make it more in keeping with Willow Bend's heritage. But he insists that the 1950s are part of our heritage, too. Well, I *know* that, but he's not taking my point, that's all."

She sighed.

"It's just that I get so excited, Gracie! Imagine 'Abe's Deli' written in those ornate gilt letters . . . and inside, horsehair couches, and delicate upholstered stools at walnut tables— or those heavy oak ones, with a pedestal support that divides into four sets of talons clutching glass balls? Can't you just see it in your mind's eye? I know I can."

Gracie loved Abe's exactly the way it was, but she didn't want to squelch Cordelia's enthusiasm. "It sounds lovely, but more appropriate for someone like you, than Abe—don't you agree? I can't quite see Abe wearing spats and a waistcoat."

Cordelia changed the subject. "You've probably come to see the journal."

"I'd like that." While Cordelia went inside to fetch it, Gracie recalled that Charlie Harris, Cordelia's longtime boarder and good friend, was off visiting distant cousins in Georgia.

When Cordelia returned, it was not with the journal, however, but with a tray bearing two tall frosted glasses that held green and white striped straws, and mint leaves resting at the rims.

"I know how you love my special concoction," Cordelia said.

"Thanks. You couldn't have pleased me more."

"And the crescents are lemony, as well." Cordelia handed Gracie a cut-glass dish holding dainty cookies dusted with confectioner's sugar. "I baked them yesterday,"

Nibbling, Gracie said, "Did you get to the auction at all?"

Cordelia looked momentarily regretful. "I was much, much too busy! There are so many guests now—weekends especially—with the nice weather about to end. And Charlie not here to help. And I've been working on some . . . some plans—" She looked thoughtful for an instant, then said briskly, "But I'm not ready to talk about them. When you're done with that, we can go inside."

Gracie obediently drank up.

Cordelia's latest treasures were kept carefully behind curved glass in an antique china closet. Cordelia fished the key from her pocket and opened the door carefully. "You'll understand, I hope, when I say look but don't touch. If the paper's as old as I'm certain it is, it will crumble easily."

"Of course." Gracie craned her neck to look in. The journal lay open, so it was difficult to guess its binding except for the slim edging. It might be leather; if so, it was preserved remarkably well. Or it might be some synthetic material imitating leather. The pages were slightly yellowed, and the script written in heavy pencil.

"Not as ornate as much of the penmanship was back then," Cordelia pointed out, "but I suspect it was written by a very young girl—perhaps even unschooled. She would have been if she was an escaping slave. Masters were supposed to keep them uneducated."

Gracie had the greatest admiration and respect for the dignity of those long-ago men and women who had endured such conditions in her very own country. However, she felt anger, too, on their behalf.

"Thank goodness those days are gone!" Cordelia said.

"When I think of how African Americans were treated!" Gracie agreed, saying more than she meant to. "Strong, beautiful men and women like Rick and Comfort Harding . . . and children, as well. Snatched from their homeland, crammed into foul slave ships and carried to a nation that would break their spirits and punish their bodies—"

"Gracie! I didn't know you had such—such passion!"

Gracie admitted, "There are some subjects that really rile me."

"I understand." Cordelia returned her attention to the contents of the china closet. "On the next shelf down. . ."

There lay a small bundle, wrapped in an obviously old piece of cloth. Its weave was loose, its colors "bleeding"—as improperly set dyes would have done. The fabric might very well have been hand spun.

"What do you think?" Cordelia's voice was low.

"You'd have to have the . . . bones. . . ."

"Carbon-dated, do you suppose? Or the fabric—"

"Of course the fabric could have been old when it was used as a shroud."

"Oh, don't you think they would have used something more respectful? I mean, we'd not bury Gooseberry or my Wendell in rags or something soiled."

Gracie shivered. She didn't want to imagine that anything might ever happen to her feline friend. Of course it would have to at some point in time. She understood that.

"Death is a natural part of life," Cordelia said, as if reading her mind. "We have to accept it when it comes. But if they went to this trouble, they probably cared enough to choose a suitable fabric." She closed the glass door carefully, then locked and tested it.

"Still, it seems what I love most of all is inanimate—this house and its history." She turned to face Gracie. "Well, now you've seen them. Let's go back to the porch, and I'll get some more lemonade. You can go home and think further about the affair of the baffling bones."

MONDAY MORNING DAWNED CLEAR and heady with a dew-laden, flower-scented breeze. Gracie inhaled deeply three times, then began a series of stretches. Gooseberry watched her, but seemed to prefer his own intensely supple versions.

"Show-off!" she muttered. Flicking his tail, Gooseberry trotted down the porch steps, looked back, and waited. "I'm coming," she called to him.

It was a perfect day for a praise-walk. Gracie adjusted her earphones and accommodated her pace to a series of spirited Gaither choruses.

At such times, she felt a kinship with the psalmist David, strumming his harp while surrounded only by the whisper of a breeze and the muted murmurs of a rocky stream. Occasionally, a lamb might interrupt with a strident bleat . . .

or a lizard, scampering on a ridge, might dislodge a tiny avalanche of sand and pebbles. But to be alone with his thoughts, his flock and his God. . . . Was it any wonder that his life seemed composed wholly of praise and prayer?

We've made a mistake, haven't we, Lord—forgetting the importance of solitude? How difficult to separate Your still, small voice from the rumble of engines and the buzz of television, to concentrate on You when daily life constantly interrupts. Not impossible, of course, since nothing is impossible with You, but—

Silencing even the tape, she tried to imagine Moses receiving his message at a busy intersection, with assorted shrieks of alarm and warning and a policeman whistling a stop to traffic while some helpful trucker aimed his fire extinguisher at the burning bush, and nearing sirens whined and blipped.

Or Jesus pleading with His Father in Central Park, while joggers thudded by and rollerbladers trailed boom-boxed rap music. When she visited Arlen and his family in New York, they always took her into the park's vast greenness, yet she found it impossible to forget the skyscrapers huddled around its circumference.

Thank You, Lord, for the coziness of Willow Bend, for the peace of this moment, for the calm in my spirit. She breathed deeply of the mingled fragrances, like a floral stew prepared by a master chef to nourish the soul. Languidly, she searched her mind for areas of concern, and found none so pressing that they couldn't wait an hour or so.

Everything was in readiness even for her next scheduled catering job. As soon as she finished her praise-walk, she'd begin the baking. Gracie liked to be prepared.

At that very moment, however, she became aware of someone moving swiftly toward her, in unmistakable haste and concern. It was Nancyalma!

Gracie felt a small clutch of dread in her heart. The money! Something had happened to the money! She snatched off her earphones.

"Oh, Gracie! You'll never believe—"

Her friend was in such obvious distress that Gracie felt compelled to put her arm around the plump shoulders. "Whatever it is, dear, it's nothing that can't be fixed—with God's help."

"I do hope you're right!" Nancyalma pulled a tissue from one apron pocket and twisted it to shreds. "No one will ever trust me again."

Gracie patted her arm. "Just tell me what's happened. Please."

"I've forgotten where I put it!" Nancyalma wailed. "I knew that it had to be a safe place—when Montgomery's in town he sometimes has friends over for poker," she broke off to explain, "and so I didn't even tell him where I'd put it. Oh, Gracie, it was somewhere that seemed so *sensible!* And I've been rummaging—nearly going crazy—and it just isn't *anywhere.*"

She paced a few steps before amending, "Well, of course

it's *somewhere*—I simply have no idea where! So when the bank opens . . . I'll have nothing to give them!"

Gracie didn't want to say that the bank didn't care. It was the Eternal Hope congregation and the community it created, who'd worked so hard, that she was concerned about. And then there were Patsy Clayton's hospital bills. . . .

"But I've interrupted your walk, and I know how important that is to you. And you have a catering job coming up, don't you?"

Actually two different ones, Gracie thought—and felt a twinge of panic. But she reassured Nancyalma, "They're under control."

Much as she hated cutting off the Lord when they'd scarcely begun talking, she needed to handle this most upsetting crisis pronto.

"You're certain—"

Nancyalma dealt with Gracie's fear before it could be spoken. "There was no theft," she stated firmly. "I made the house safer than Fort Knox—chairs braced under doorknobs. Windows locked. I even set booby-traps here and there—piles of books that would topple easily. Kettles and wind-chimes where no one creeping around could expect them. And I slept lightly. I'd have heard a moth flutter."

What about your brother? Gracie wanted to ask, but didn't dare.

Once again, Nancyalma preempted the concern.

"Monty helped me search, until he had to leave to meet some friends. He offered to bring them all back—but I reminded him we don't have workman's compensation." She laughed weakly. "That was a joke—in case someone broke a leg . . . or neck on my clutter. . . . Oh, Gracie!" she finished shakily, "wouldn't you think I'd remember something this important? Wouldn't you expect that at my age I'd have learned . . . some . . . some organization?"

Actually, Gracie often forgot where she'd put small things, minutes after setting them down. But she couldn't imagine misplacing something so important as the Eternal Hope auction money. It was their contribution to Patsy Clayton's future, their way of thanking her for her indomitable spirit.

She was grateful that in her house there was "a place for everything and everything in its place," though she wasn't fanatical enough to fuss when Uncle Miltie left his ceramic glazes by the bathroom sink or tracked wood shavings across her just-scrubbed kitchen floor.

She might shudder a bit at the latter. Then she'd remind herself that he wouldn't produce wood shavings at all if he didn't do so many odd jobs around the house.

But I do have a hard time, Lord, she admitted, *understanding how anyone can be as*—she struggled for a noncondemnatory term—*organizationally challenged as Nancyalma is. Help me to sympathize . . . or even help! This is deeply serious.*

Though, secretly—and just as sincerely—she believed that,

when it came to Nancyalma's chaotic housekeeping style, she was probably past helping. Anyone who designated areas of her house as "The Landfill," "Recycling Center," and "Toxic Dump" was surely beyond rehabilitation. Aladdin's cave, indeed!

As they passed Estelle Livett's house, they heard her practicing her scales.

Nancyalma shuddered. "Did she really study with some famous teacher and sing professionally?"

"She says so," Gracie answered diplomatically, "but I've never been tempted to check her résumé."

Nancyalma covered her ears and hurried ahead, calling back, "Why can't she close her doors and windows when she's practicing?"

Gracie hadn't the heart to point out that they *were* closed. Projection was one of Estelle's undeniable strengths.

Waiting for Gracie to catch up, Nancyalma had thought better of her critical stance. "At least so early in the morning," she said, modifying her tone.

Bert Benton and Polly, his wife, were taking a post-breakfast tour of their flower beds. Each held a pair of secaturs.

"Your roses are still beautiful!" Gracie told them. Loud music issued from an upstairs window.

Bert called back, "Can't hear you!"

"Roses!" Gracie shouted. "Beautiful!"

He shook his head in frustration. "Barry!" he shouted at the window. "Turn it down!"

The volume went up, its drumbeats so pronounced that Gracie's nerves bounced in syncopation.

"That kid!" Bert excused himself and sprinted into the house. Moments later, the music stopped. Soon the door banged open, and young Barry stomped out.

He glared at Gracie and Nancyalma. Then his mother instructed him, "Tell Mrs. Parks and Mrs. Smith good morning. Show them you have some manners."

He did as he was told, but with obvious ill grace. It was with relief that the two women left the Benton family to their morning activities.

𝒫

Two hours later, Gracie entered her house to find Uncle Miltie eating a late breakfast while a muted "Magnum PI" rerun played on the television in the other room.

"I can get back to my chair for the car chase," he informed her. "Could I interest you in a blueberry pancake or two?"

"*Hmmm* . . ." Sinking onto a stool, she rested her chin in her hands.

"Tired already?" A frown creased his forehead.

She nodded.

"Maybe you should cut down on your mileage?"

"*Hmmm . . .*" She realized Uncle Miltie hadn't any idea what had been detaining her.

Sifting through those heaps of papers . . . those plastic containers, cardboard boxes and grocery bags—Did You notice, Lord, that some of those magazines were from five years back? I can see saving the Guideposts—*I do that, too—but the outdated coupons?*

"*I know your every thought, your going out and coming in. . . .*" Usually that knowledge was blanket-warm to her heart; now her cheeks burned. "*And yet you are my beloved child!*" Was she being too hard on poor Nancyalma?

Lord, I don't deserve Your love—none of us do. None of us can. It's only through Your grace—

"So what's wrong, Gracie?" Uncle Miltie's voice was tense. "You've got more *hmmm's* than a tuning fork!"

Gracie tugged herself from her thoughts. Old sweetie pie that he was, she had to let him know what was going on. At the same time, she couldn't bear to see how upset he would be. There was no middle ground with George Morgan.

"I'm just being silly," she said, mentally crossing her fingers.

"You wouldn't know how, and you know it!"

She forced a smile. "I could learn." She reached to pat his arm. "Really, dear Uncle Miltie, there's not a thing wrong that won't be cured by your blueberry pancakes—"

She suddenly broke off, springing to her feet to help rescue the burning flapjacks. Moments later both she and Uncle

Miltie were collapsed into laughter and one another's arms.

"*Crêpes brulées*," Gracie told him. "Second cousin to *crème brulée*. You did it on purpose!"

"Speaking of bumblebees," Uncle Miltie gasped when they had nearly caught their breath.

"I didn't know we were!"

"We were about to. Why do you suppose they're called that?"

She knew she was going to welcome this distraction.

"Bumble," he said, starting more pancake batter. "What does that mean, exactly? When Adam named the bumblebee, did he really mean *bunglebee*?"

Gracie said drily, "I don't believe they spoke much English in the Garden of Eden."

"Think of it, Gracie!" He gestured, flecks of batter flying off his wooden spoon. "In the insect world they're like the Goodyear blimp among ultralights! Now *dragonfly* I can understand. He drags that long tail behind him—'drag-on-fly'— got it? So that fits, I suppose."

He waited for affirmation.

Gracie watched as he sprinkled blueberries into the new batch of mix.

He harrumphed. "And if we assume that yes, Adam did refer to the cumbersomeness of the bumblebee—"

"Is *cumbersomeness* a real word? And wouldn't that make it a *cumberbee*?"

He banged the bowl on the counter. "Cook your own pancakes!" His eyebrows twitched. "You're getting more like
Marge every day!"

"I'm sorry, Uncle Miltie. Please do go on with your natural
history lecture. It's just that today—"

"I knew something was wrong!" he crowed. He came to
sit beside her.

"First, though, about the bumblebees?" Gracie still was
reluctant to share her news.

He sighed. "It was just a dumb joke."

"I like your dumb jokes!"

She reached out to hug him. He beamed at her. "I know
you do, my girl."

He paused. "It's just that while dragonflies seem somewhat aptly named, and we can make a case for bunglebees—
we can't escape the conclusion that Adam was dyslexic."

"How so?" she asked dutifully.

"Butterflies. There's no stretch that makes that work! He
had to mean—"

"Flutterbys!" they said together.

Uncle Miltie pecked her on the cheek. "Now let me make
you some of those pancakes!"

Lord, she prayed, as her precious octogenarian worked
happily, *how I love him. How I praise You for enriching my life
with his company. He is so gifted in the qualities that matter—
love, generosity, compassion—that we who care so much for him*

can easily accept his comedy routines. But—honestly, Lord—don't even You sometimes wince at some of those terrible jokes?

"There!" Uncle Miltie set before her a plate of perfect pancakes, golden brown and oozing tiny rivulets of berry juice.

"My compliments to the chef!" Gracie said, and dug in.

Fortunately, Gracie's baking efforts were more gratifying than her praise-walk. By dinnertime, she could go nowhere in the house or yard without inhaling the satisfying fragrances of chocolate, cinnamon or caramelized brown sugar. The next morning, these aromas would give way to tantalizing scents of onion, sage, basil and fresh-cut fruits—but now, baking done, she could with an uncluttered conscience prepare a light meal, then make her way to choir practice.

Leftover hamloaf with mustard sauce on whole wheat buns and coleslaw left Uncle Miltie looking replete. Gracie's own appetite was affected by her worry—but her uncle seemed not to have noticed.

"Some fruit?" Gracie asked. "I've got some nice sliced pineapple."

Uncle Miltie held up his hands for a time-out.

"Later, then," she suggested. She kissed the top of his head, gave Gooseberry a farewell pat and headed out in her old blue Cadillac, Fannie Mae. A full five minutes early, Gracie was climbing the creaky steps to Eternal Hope's choir loft.

Amy Cantrell arrived breathless. "Hello there," she sang out as she took her seat in the front row of the soprano section.

"Your limp seems better."

"Mrs. Glass had some ointment—I don't know what was in it." She flexed her ankle. "Just as long as it works! Right?"

"Then Sophie's still here?"

"Just for a few—" Amy broke off as Barb's baton tapped authoritatively—official notification that practice would begin on time as usual. The gathered singers, all in their places now, looked expectant.

"—more weeks."

"*Shhhh!*" hissed Estelle, her warning a lot louder than Amy's low whisper.

But Amy wasn't finished yet. "Long enough, she hopes, to convince her brother—" She broke off as Barb hit a raucous chord.

But Gracie could guess what was coming. The "Get Abe Moved to Florida Campaign" was still in full swing.

8

SINCE NANCYALMA hadn't been at practice and hadn't phoned an excuse to Barb, Gracie decided to swing by on the way home.

The small house, tucked among maples and oaks near the edge of town, showed light at every window. No car was parked in the narrow gravel driveway, so Gracie assumed that Monty had taken Nancyalma's car on some venture or other. And Nancyalma herself undoubtedly still frantically searched for the missing money amidst the sea of her tumbled-together possessions.

Gracie took a moment to pray not only for the speedy recovery of the money, but for her friend's recovered peace of mind. Only then did she get out of her car and walk through the tall grass to the cranberry-colored front door where a wrought-iron shepherd's hook supported a hanging basket of diplodemia. As she had on her earlier visit, Gracie admired its large pink blossoms and trailing foliage.

The door opened almost immediately.

"Oh! Gracie! I'm so glad you're here!"

"When you weren't at choir practice—"

"How could I? I simply couldn't face them! They'd ask about the money." She paused, her voice quavering. "Did they? Ask about the money? If I'd remembered to deposit it?"

"Not a word," Gracie assured her. "Would you like me to help you for a half hour or so?"

"Please." Nancyalma led the way, stepping over fallen stacks of books, allowing Gracie to follow her through the congestion by the best routes. They entered a small spare bedroom.

"And sewing room," Nancyalma explained, waving toward a clutter of fabric heaped on the bed and a sewing machine nearly hidden beneath clothing stacked for mending. She stood for a moment, her shoulders slumping.

"Oh, Gracie!" she wailed. "I get so disgusted with myself, so discouraged—" Her voice broke.

"When this happens, when I'm on one of these search-and-discover missions, I dig like a madwoman. I talk to myself, I talk to God—not even listening for an answer. I want to promise Him I'll never get into a mess like this again. But I can't bring myself to promise something I know is impossible."

"With God all things are—"

"Oh, I know. I know!" Nancyalma snapped, uncharacteristically. "Nothing's impossible for *Him*—just for me!" Her lower lip wobbled. Gracie eyed the mess in front of her and took a deep breath.

Nancyalma dabbed at her eyes with a corner of her none-too-clean apron.

Gracie hugged her. "You're not alone, you know. You have me and all your friends in the choir. And we all have the Lord." Almost as an afterthought, she added, "And there's Monty."

Nancyalma pulled away. "Oh, yes," she sighed. "There's Monty."

An hour later, Gracie went home—after extracting from Nancyalma her promise to give up for the night, take a long, hot bath, and go to bed.

They had found a long-lost passport, a notebook of family recipes Nancyalma had thought forever vanished, and some antique pewter candlesticks she had wrapped for safekeeping and stored in an old breadbox beneath a bed.

Uncle Miltie waited with a boiling kettle and a cup complete with teabag. "Money still missing?" Much as she'd hated having to distress him, Gracie had finally revealed the problem of the vanished cash before she'd left for choir practice. Then, not waiting for an answer, he asked, "You think maybe it's already gone?"

It was a possibility she'd rather not entertain. She thought aloud, "If he—if it had been stolen, wouldn't he be long gone?"

"Not if he's smart." Uncle Miltie perched on a stool, looking pensive. "If I was going to rob a bank, for instance, I'd stash the loot and then pretend to work harder than anybody else to discover the culprit. Wouldn't you?"

Since she had never considered robbing a bank—or anything else—she had no idea.

"Pretty clever, huh? Him working up that sweat, pulling in more and more money—and all the while—"

"We don't know that," she chided him gently.

"No," he admitted, "we don't. And we don't know we won't find Santa Claus stuck in our chimney come morning." He opened the screen door, allowing the night breeze to enter. "Still, it's a safe bet."

Long before lunchtime, everything was in readiness for the late-afternoon catering event, which was a celebration for the Searfosses. Recent brief hospital stays had coincided with their wedding anniversary. Anna, whose diabetes had severely damaged her sight, had been in for tests only, while Joe had undergone treatment following removal of several suspicious-looking growths on his shoulders and back. It had been Cordelia Fountain who'd suggested a welcome-home get-together, with Gracie commissioned to supply delicious eats.

Anna had her heart set on having friends and neighbors at their own home, so it was there they would gather.

Entertainment was to be provided by Cordelia's reading from her mysterious journal—as a sort of an "appetizer," she said, for the Historical Society gala at the end of the month.

Unstoppable Cordelia, thought Gracie. She seemed to have an insatiable appetite for attention. *What is it, Lord,* she asked in her thoughts, *that causes some of us to reach out for publicity, even notoriety?* Yet it wasn't only Cordelia—think how Rocky beamed when one of his editorials received favorable feedback! Or how Uncle Miltie expanded when she applauded his handyman expertise—or even how she herself warmed to praise of a specially prepared dish. *We're all the same, aren't we, Lord—easy prey to pride?*

Uncle Miltie and Gooseberry paused by the screen door and sniffed deeply. "Cold chicken pie," Uncle Miltie guessed. "Cranberry chutney? Candied sweet potatoes? Chocolate . . . something!" He eased inside. "You, my dear, are my very favorite niece!"

"What if I were to tell you this is all for the party? That we're having bologna sandwiches for lunch?"

He chuckled. "I know you better than that, Gracie, my girl!"

Marge tapped at the door, opening it even as she called, "I came to help pack!"

Uncle Miltie snorted. "Funny you got here right at lunchtime."

Gracie laughed. "We have enough bologna for another sandwich, Marge. Have a seat!"

"Bologna sandwiches?" Marge threw Gracie a look of admiration. "You'd make even that a gourmet experience, Gracie! Add some outlandish spice or relish and *voilà!* Another triumph!" She rummaged around, coming up with a tin of potato chips. "Everything ready for this afternoon?"

"Even the favors!"

"I'm impressed."

"Me, too," Gracie admitted. "It was almost too easy— scary. Maybe I've forgotten something crucial—or substituted salt for sugar."

"You never could," Marge said loyally, "or if you did, it would start a trend."

Gracie smiled wryly. "I've just got a lot on my mind."

"The money." Marge helped herself to a chip. And another. She handed the tin to Uncle Miltie. "When you told me, I thought I'd have a heart attack."

"I know where the money is." He waved a pickle slice. "Or at least who has it."

"Not Montgomery! Not that handsome and available man! Be still, my heart!" Marge joked. "Besides, we keep realizing, don't we, that he'd be an idiot to spirit away Patsy's money when he's our only real suspect? Maybe it's time to tell Herb about this?" She was referring to Willow Bend's police chief.

"I think calling Herb is a fine idea," volunteered Uncle Miltie. Spearing another pickle, he asked, "How *do* you tell the difference between a cucumber and a crocodile?"

Marge rolled her eyes. Then she asked, "How do you tell the difference . . . between a cucumber and a crocodile?"

"Don't you want to guess?"

She sighed. "Well, they both have bumps. And they're both green. A cucumber doesn't have legs and a tail?"

"Way off," he chuckled. "Guess again."

"One's a veggie and the other's a reptile?"

"Give up?"

"Please," begged Marge.

Gracie nodded.

Uncle Miltie leaned back in his chair. Eyes sparkling, he said, "You bite a pickle, and a crocodile bites you!"

"But then if it's dill, the pickle bites you back!" Marge added.

Uncle Miltie sniffed, "I said *cucumber*, not *pickle*!" He looked to Gracie for confirmation, but all she said was, "That was one of your better ones, dear. Could I interest you in pie?"

9

IT WAS A MULTI-FRUIT CONCOCTION, oozing colored juices, with cinnamon and sugar sprinkled over the crust.

"*Ummm.*" Marge closed her eyes, savoring the first bite. "Apple. Peach. Pear." She frowned, poking beneath the crust. "Raspberry and strawberry?"

Not waiting for a response, she asked, "Had you heard about Abe?"

"What about Abe?" Uncle Miltie snapped.

"Is that grape?" Marge asked. "Gracie, it *can't* be!"

"What—about—Abe?" Uncle Miltie ground each word through gritted teeth.

"Oh. Flu, Sophie thinks. She says he's come down with it all of a sudden, and is having a hard time getting out of bed."

Uncle Miltie laid down his fork. "Been there. You just have to tough it out."

"Really?" Marge asked. "Why, George Morgan, I didn't think any virus would dare bother you!"

He seemed to be trying to ignore her, but curiosity got the better of him. "How's that?" he muttered.

"You might tell it one of your jokes," she said sweetly. "It wouldn't stick around for a second one."

Gracie, meanwhile, had tuned both of them out and gone to the Lord. *Please,* she prayed, *touch Abe's body with healing.* Later, she'd take him some of the party foods. Sophie would already have made chicken soup.

Anna sipped orange juice at a small white wrought-iron table. Cordelia whispered, "Anna wanted to help, but I made her sit down. She was fading out." She shook her head. "She's always been one of my favorites, ever since she was at the library."

Gracie was unloading her bowls and platters onto the largest table—draped in summery blue and festooned with oversized bows. Balloons bobbed in a breeze that would have been scarcely noticeable, otherwise.

"Her love of books is part of what makes her so special. By the way, have you seen Joe?"

"He went to cut chrysanthemums. I do hope he shakes any bugs off."

"Uncle Miltie would say, 'What's a picnic without bugs?'"

"I thought it was ants. That would be true if peonies were in season," Cordelia raised an eyebrow. "Surely you prepared more food than this!"

"Marge and Uncle Miltie will be along soon. And I have more in the car." She knew Cordelia liked to micromanage, and her meddling always was with a good heart. Still, Gracie allowed herself to count to three.

Suddenly, Cordelia looked beyond Gracie and scolded, "Anna, you sit right down! We can manage very well. And what kind of anniversary party will it be if you decide to take a trip to the emergency room?"

"Oh, Cordelia, how you do fuss!" But Anna obediently returned to her seat—a bit shakily, Gracie noticed, as she saw Cordelia take her arm.

Thank You, Lord, for showing me so clearly once again that Cordelia has a loving heart. So often she seems focused only on herself and her house and its history. Yet she cares about Anna, just as we all do. After all, she was the one who planned this whole day!

However, before Gracie could take herself to task for a continuing tendency to be judgmental, Cordelia said, "I do hope everyone comes. I know that they'll be enthralled to hear excerpts from the journal. Finding such artifacts is so important, Gracie! Surely you agree! Not just for the sake of my business, but as a boon for Willow Bend itself. Think of what can happen once word gets out of this additional proof of *our* involvement in the Underground Railroad!"

To avoid saying something that might upset Cordelia or, worse yet, seem to encourage her persistent publicity-seeking, Gracie excused herself.

As she continued to set up, she carried on chatting with her best friend. *Forgive me, Lord, but it's easy enough for Cordelia to take credit for the long-ago reality of the Underground Railroad now, when we live in a world where our courage isn't tested—*

She broke off, shamed by such easy judgment. Better to worry about her need to get those appetizers ready before Marge and Uncle Miltie arrived with the rest.

"And besides," Cordelia continued, "I've already asked Anna to try writing a script based on the journal, and she promised to think it over. We truly must keep her well, mustn't we? And busy? That means being involved. Wouldn't a play be marvelous for the Sesquitennial?"

Gracie protested, "But that's not for years—"

"We should start now, shouldn't we? Getting ourselves ready for when it comes?"

≈

It was a lovely party. Many attending brought copies of Anna's charming Lazy Lake books—which had been redis-covered and republished—to be autographed. Adjusting her thick glasses and using a magnifying glass, Anna scrawled laboriously, but never paused in her chatter—exchanging kind words with everyone while Joe stood just behind her, one hand lightly on her shoulder.

Though childless, they obviously loved children. And each other. Together, opening gifts and cutting the cake, the Searfosses glowed. Then, when Rocky arrived to take a photo himself for the paper, the pair cuddled like newlyweds.

Gracie felt a tug at her heart. Elmo's accident had robbed her of such an extended love. *I wonder, Lord, if I'll ever get past that sharp thrust of pain that catches me unaware. Usually, now, I think of El with warmth—even with humor. I can move myself past the grief. But sometimes—*

She dabbed a tissue to her eyes—surreptitiously, she thought—but in moments Uncle Miltie and Rocky had converged on her, one to a side. *Lord, please don't let them say anything comforting, or I'll blubber all over the celebration.*

She needn't have worried.

Uncle Miltie patted her hand, assuring her that she'd outdone herself with the canapés.

And Rocky caught her other arm and said, "They're playing our song."

She didn't hear any music, and said so.

He clucked. "You don't hear those windchimes hanging from the apple tree? Maybe somewhere a bird is singing. . . . Gooseberry is certainly listening with rapt attention."

"Gooseberry," she said wryly, "is thinking of scattering feathers, rather than humming along."

"Then don't we have a duty—to remove him from temptation and save the aviary? Why don't the three of us take an afternoon walk?"

She protested, "The clean-up—"

"If anything's left," Uncle Miltie said, "Marge and I can manage."

"Of course we can!" chided Marge. "You guys run along now."

"And don't hurry back! I want you to lose track of how many of those meringues I consume."

"Five so far," Uncle Miltie chuckled. "I'll keep count for you, Gracie!"

It was during the flurry of picture-taking, just as Gracie, Rocky and Gooseberry were leaving, that another gift appeared—unwrapped.

Joe discovered it and took it to Anna. "It's one of those lovely little wax carvings," he said, "like the ones somebody left at the hospital."

And at the auction, too, Gracie remembered. And later for Amy, when she was limping.

Anna took it gently into her hands, running her fingertips over its smoothness, then turning it over. "Is it marked with the same initials?"

Joe examined the base of the carving. "Just the same. N.A.M.S. I wonder who that could be?"

Gracie wondered, too.

And she was even more baffled when, that evening, she took a plate of goodies over to Abe. Sophie accepted it with a broad smile.

"Luckily, I've made as many good friends in Florida as Abe has here. Well, bring it on in, Gracie. He'll want to thank you himself."

Abe, cocooned in blankets, waved weakly from the couch. On a small table nearby—among a clutter of crumpled tissues, glasses of juice and water, and a large bottle of aspirin—stood a carved wax candle. An owl.

The next day, as she recuperated from one catering event and planned for the next, Gracie explored the possibilities. No matter how she scoured her mind, she could come up with no one who had four initials. A few could claim NAS or NMS—including Nancyalma—and there was even one NAM. But—

And suddenly it hit her. Nancyalma—if the two names were separated—could qualify, after all! Nancy Alma Montgomery Smith. NAMS. How had it not occurred to her before?

She attempted to picture Nancyalma painstakingly designing and producing the small creatures. She'd seen no evidence of such effort, but how could a person know everything that grab-bag of a house contained?

Uncle Miltie—entering with a bouquet of Queen Anne's lace—said, "You look like Gooseberry when he's sampled the baking."

"NAMS," she said slowly. "I believe I've figured it out."

He trimmed the stems of the wild carrot, putting them in a tall vase.

And she told him.

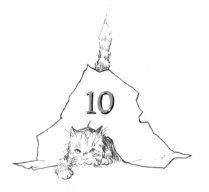

MOST CATERING EVENTS were culinary adventures—but this one, Gracie felt, fitted better into the ordeal category. Bert Benton was a good businessman, a nice guy, and a better-than-average baritone. His wife Polly could hold her own in the Mason City courthouse, where she served as public defender. But Gracie knew no one who would compliment the Bentons on their son, Barry. He was a poster child for brattiness.

Gracie had never actually seen him tease the neighborhood pets, but that might only prove just how sneaky he really was. After all, whenever he walked past, Gooseberry hissed and Charlotte, Marge's Shih Tzu, growled. Sometimes, even, both of them growled. The fact remained that, confused as Gooseberry might sometimes be about his species, she trusted his instincts. If he hissed or growled at someone, that someone had *earned* her cat's hostility.

Don Delano, dedicated high school teacher, had even once confided that he considered early retirement only when he thought of Barry one day entering his classroom.

So here Gracie was, in the secondary stages of preparing to cater a party celebrating Barry's twelfth birthday.

"I guess what we're really celebrating," Polly Benton had explained when first talking to Gracie, "is that we've all three made it this far without anyone committing murder. Though I won't say it hasn't been considered."

Gracie strained for something good to say. "He . . . seems very much his own person."

Polly nodded. "That's kind of you. Anyway, we do love him and keep hoping each different stage is the last."

Gracie yearned to help. But how could she, without pointing out that Barry was somewhat spoiled by both his busy parents.

Certainly, Gracie didn't feel that every woman's place was at home cooking and sewing. It was simply that the working wife and mother always has two full-time jobs. At least. And usually something had to give.

The silence was getting thick. Polly gave Gracie an optimistic grin and a thumbs-up. Gracie knew she loved her son.

Gracie nodded. "Believe me, even Arlen Parks was never a saint. Far from it, at times."

Polly laughed.

Gracie did think to herself, Barry might have benefited from some early well-placed swats to the too young rear. Just as Arlen had. Instead, she said, "Parenting is on-the-job training, start to finish. Unfortunately, no manual comes with the product. We just do the best we can, and leave the rest up to God."

"I'm afraid God is tired of hearing about Barry," his mother quipped.

"God wants us to share our concerns—not only with Him, but with one another. Please, any time you need to talk, I'm here. He's never tired of hearing about any of us, and neither am I."

Polly smiled. "So now we need to talk about the party. Barry has made up a menu. I know how you like to experiment, make your dishes more exciting. And I love your cooking, I really do. But Barry. . ."

". . . is just a boy," Gracie said.

"And Barry said—" Another sigh. "No 'fancy sissy stuff'— his words—like balloons and streamers and 'cutesy favors.' Oh, and no cake. He hates cake. He wants chocolate chip cookies and brownies. Without nuts. And no ice cream, except in the double-thick chocolate shakes."

Okay," Gracie told her. "This is pretty normal for the age group." Fast-food junkies, the lot of them, she added to herself.

"There's one more thing." Polly spoke quickly now.

Gracie nodded, encouraging her friend to go on.

"He—Barry—he wants you just to drop off the food before the guests arrive—and wait until they're gone to clean up."

Gracie nodded again. Nothing out of the way about that.

"He doesn't want us there, either. Bert and me."

Gracie had thought that her opinion of Barry Benton could sink no lower.

She'd been wrong.

Lord, I do appreciate how You balance the negatives with unexpected joy. Overbalance, actually!

Having added chocolate chunks to replace the texture the nuts should have provided, Gracie gave the brownie batter a final stir and poured it into the baking dish. Perched on a stool, her walker leaning against a table leg, sat Patsy Clayton.

"I just love to watch you bake!" Patsy hugged herself. "I can hardly believe that all that stuff goes together to make something as yummy as cookies. It's kind of magic, don't you think?"

Gracie smiled. "There's a lot of 'magic' in the world—though I prefer to think of it as God's blessing."

"You mean God invented chocolate chip cookies, too? Besides planets and oceans and stuff? How did He have the *time?*"

Gracie slid the baking dish into the oven and set the timer.

"Sometimes He gives the ideas to the people He created. Then they take it from there."

"That's even better, isn't it? That makes us—sort of partners with Him. Doesn't it?"

"Such a lovely way to express it, dear!"

"It makes me feel warm and cuddly, knowing God loves us."

"Me, too."

"And your brownies are the best!"

These wouldn't be, Gracie knew. No hint of almond flavoring. No macadamia nuts. Not even walnuts or pecans. Whoever said "The customer is always right" had never met Barry Benton.

For a moment, the only sounds were the ticking of the timer and Uncle Miltie's snoring from the couch.

"Do you think God can go everywhere?" Patsy's voice was low and expressionless.

"Of course, dear!" Gracie drew up a stool and lightly rested her arm across Patsy's shoulders. "Was there somewhere you thought He might not want to go?"

"I thought they might not allow Him."

"Who, Patsy? And where?"

"In the operating room." Her voice shook. "He wouldn't be scrubbed or anything, and you know—the mask and gloves. They might not have any to fit."

"Dear Patsy! He'll be there right with you!"

"And they won't even know it?"

Gracie paused thoughtfully. "Some of them will. Some of the doctors and nurses know Him every bit as well as we do. They'll be praying before the surgery . . . and even during it."

"When I'm asleep and can't pray."

"And God will be holding You all the time, telling you how much He loves you."

Patsy said, "I shouldn't be scared, should I? I've done this so often."

"It's only natural to be a little bit afraid, dear."

"This isn't a little bit, though. This is a lot!" Another sigh. "Mama will be so disappointed if it doesn't work this time."

"And you," Gracie said softly, "will you be very disappointed, too?"

Patsy shrugged. "Actually, getting around would seem funny without my walker."

Wordlessly, Gracie hugged her.

If mess indicated a successful birthday party, then Barry's had been an unqualified triumph. The food table was overturned, one of Gracie's pewter trays dented, and two plastic lawn chairs—the stackable kind—broken beyond hope of repair. In the accumulation of debris littering the lawn, crumpled paper napkins and blobs of food joined styrofoam plates and cups that looked as though they'd been ripped apart by mastiffs.

There had obviously been a food fight; more than one hamburger patty, bleeding catsup and mustard, clung to the brick of the house, while other spatters attested to further "hits."

Uncle Miltie, who had come with Gracie for the pick-up, stood in shock for a full two minutes before saying, "Be happy this was a party you were invited *not* to attend."

What a contrast—Gracie shared with the Lord, as she began gathering unused, unspoiled food—what little there was—*this undisciplined boy and dear, sweet Patsy. Surely it's true that adversity builds character. I wonder, Lord, would it be out of line to pray for a little character-building adversity for Barry Benton? I feel so sorry for his parents! They're such pleasant people, and well-meaning. But they remind me of nonswimmers who wade out too far and find themselves caught in an undertow.*

I wouldn't want to pray for anything really horrible to happen to Barry, but if You can think of something minor, not life-threatening, just enough to wake him up to how blessed he is—

She broke off, suddenly remembering what author Lurlene McDaniel had said to a group of teenaged fans—that while we can't choose what life brings to us, we can choose how we react to it. Barry, Gracie thought, was a nice kid who'd developed a lot of bad habits. Somewhere, though, that niceness was just biding its time.

11

GRACIE WAS LYING on the sofa, Gooseberry spread across her feet like very warm, very fuzzy bedroom slippers. He was breathing heavily, rhythmically. Occasionally his paws began twitching, scraping thin air.

"What are you chasing?" Gracie asked quietly. "Or whom?" Gooseberry had been known, on occasion, to think himself a watch-cat. When one paperboy adamantly refused to come nearer than the front sidewalk, Gracie wondered what had gotten into her usually mild-mannered cat. He'd never minded the newspaper before—often even "fetched" it.

But then she'd seen the boy take careful aim—not at the front porch, but at Gooseberry. Come to think of it, could that have been Barry? He'd delivered the paper for a short time—and that would certainly explain Gooseberry's antipathy. No doubt Charlotte had been an unwilling target, as well.

"Gracie, my dear, ready for a treat?"

Still a bit uncomfortable from dinner, Gracie nonetheless smiled up at Uncle Miltie. "How sweet." She accepted the cereal bowl heaped with ice cream and slathered with fudge topping. A maraschino cherry capped a generous swirl of whipped cream. Gracie groaned.

Uncle Miltie must have mistaken satiation for delight. "You deserve the best, Gracie," he said fondly, then carried his own bowl to his favorite chair and turned the television on with the remote.

Gooseberry stirred restlessly.

Perhaps he smelled ice cream in his dreams.

But it was the phone that woke him. As Gracie went to answer, she left her bowl within easy reach. Hoping there wouldn't be any left when she returned, she picked up the receiver.

"Oh, Gracie!" Nancyalma wailed. "I don't know what I'm going to do! I really don't! I've been over and over absolutely everything—and the money's nowhere! Could you—is there any way—I hate to even ask—" Her voice broke on a sob. "Every time the phone rings—or the doorbell—I wonder if someone's waiting with handcuffs!"

Why there had been no hue and cry over the missing money puzzled Gracie. Perhaps everyone else—like Gracie herself—cringed at the prospect of phoning Herb Bower to make it official.

The truth was, they all shared blame. Everyone knew how

chaotic Nancyalma's house was, and they should have found some way to dissuade her from taking the auction proceeds home with her.

Hurt feelings notwithstanding.

Brother, or no brother.

"What time, dear?" she asked.

"Oh, Gracie! Oh, Gracie! Really? How can I thank you? You're an absolute angel!" She sighed tremulously. "Would eight-thirty be too early?"

"I'll be there," Gracie promised.

"Who was that?" Uncle Miltie licked his spoon.

Gooseberry blissfully licked Gracie's now-empty bowl.

"Nancyalma. Would you mind if I didn't have breakfast with you tomorrow?"

"Money not found yet." It wasn't a question.

"Not yet. But it will be. I know it."

"Oh, yeah," he hooted, "but not by the two of you—not unless you search Monty's luggage." He creaked to a standing position. "Take your bowl to the kitchen?" Striving for balance, he braced against a chair.

"Let me," she offered, then leaned down and gave Gooseberry a "thank you" pat.

Next morning, when she whispered that it was time for a praise-walk, Gooseberry merely flicked an ear and curled into a ball.

Was he still weighted down by last night's dessert? Remembering the generous proportions of her sundae, she shuddered. "Better you than me," she said. "Have a nice sleep."

Actually, she looked forward to being alone—as soon as she was past traffic and sidewalks. She needed some serious time with the Lord. In the meantime, she waved or called to people she passed, threw a stick for a passing dog to fetch and paused to admire Comfort Harding's vibrant patch of zinnias.

The fragrance of fresh-mown grass filled her nostrils. Cars—on their way to work or shopping—passed, and familiar voices called greetings. Gracie watched all that she passed with her usual eager and appreciative interest. Finally, she reached the edge of town where the only sounds she heard were those soothing notes Nature made.

It was time.

Well, Lord—she began, *I need to ask for patience, for one thing. A lot of patience! Let Nancyalma never guess how frustrated I feel in her clutter. After all, I know there are things about me that annoy many people. For example, I do take sides. Estelle thinks I always agree with Barb—and I can't argue, because Barb always makes the better decisions. At least to my way of thinking, though You may see things differently.*

But she was getting off the subject.

I feel certain, Lord, You do know where that money is. Please let us find it—but in Your perfect time. Only soon.

Speaking of time—she'd better make her way to Nancyalma's house. *Amen,* she added, adjusting her headphones and putting her pace in high gear.

She had expected to find Nancyalma in the crucial stages of a panic attack. Instead, she was sprawled in one lawnchair, her feet propped on another. "I'm just catching my breath, Gracie," she said, rising.

"Brace yourself. If you thought it was bad Monday—" She allowed Gracie to precede her.

Even warned, Gracie was shocked.

"I know," Nancyalma sighed. "It looks as though a tornado came to visit and decided to stay a while." She picked her way laboriously through, followed by her guest. Old wrapping paper was stuck in encyclopedia volumes, empty cereal boxes held unmatched socks, out-of-date coupons and incomplete decks of playing cards were in coffee cans. Gracie could not imagine what had occasioned the "fresh" disarray.

Rather than less, there was certainly more.

It was mid-afternoon when they surrendered. Gracie had never known such exhaustion.

Nancyalma had given them tea and now rinsed their cups. "We need to decide the next step. Or, I suppose, I do. Well, I've thought of hiring a backhoe, practicing selective burning or moving to Argentina. But what I'm going to do instead is . . ." She drew a deep breath, then rushed on, "have a yard sale! I've asked Monty to stay and help."

"A—" It was the last thing Gracie might have expected.

"And soon. A week from Saturday, so I won't have much time to advertise. I'm desperate, Gracie. Desperate enough—*finally!*—to make a change in my life. And to do that, I have to get rid of . . . *stuff!*" She nodded briskly. "I have the motivation now, and I don't want to lose it. I've tried this before. Many times. And then I look around, and the sheer magnitude . . . the total impossibility . . . overwhelms me. But not this time.

"I don't care what my brother has planned for tomorrow. He's going to help me burn papers I haven't needed in years—just nothing green! And he can wash milkglass, kettles, even antique glass. I'm setting a goal, Gracie, to cut my load by half. At least half, maybe more. And whatever doesn't sell at the yard sale is going straight to the charity bins. I'm not going to make this jungle seem like it's one I like living in anymore!"

Sitting down, she pushed aside a heap of circulars and unopened mail. "Now," she said, "the only question is—can I follow through this time?"

Gracie caught her hand.

"Will you pray for me, Gracie?"

"You know I will!"

"It must sound so silly. There are people in the world starving to death ... people dodging bullets and grenades ... people dying of cancer and AIDS—people with real problems—and I ask God to help me with ... clutter! What's wrong with me, Gracie? How can I be so ... so paralyzed by something everyone else handles without thinking twice?" Tears welled in her eyes.

Gracie was firm in her response. "Nothing seems silly to God, dear friend. Why don't we tell Him all about it— together. Right now!"

"I don't understand," Gracie sighed, as she and Uncle Miltie did the dinner dishes, "how the weeks whiz by so quickly. Here it is, choir practice night again—and the first thing we know, it'll be another Sunday. A whole week nearly gone, and what have I accomplished?"

"Nothing much." Uncle Miltie dried a plate and added it to a Tower-of-Pisa-like stack Nancyalma would once have admired. "Just catered a birthday party, spent two days helping Nancyalma with what she calls her 'archaeological dig,' and answered every need and whim of your crochety old uncle and equally querulous cat."

Gooseberry appeared at the screen door, loudly suggesting he be admitted.

"Ever hear the one about the sword swallower who died in the middle of his act? The autopsy showed he had something stuck in his throat." He chuckled. "As if they needed a coroner to see that! Pretty sharp, huh, Gracie?"

Gracie smiled at him. It had been a fairly painless joke—except for the poor sword swallower!

"Off with you," he said, shooing her from the sink. "I'll finish. Barb'll make you sit beside Estelle if you're late. Or Marge—a fate worse than death." His grin was mischievous. "Aren't you gonna give me the party line? Tell me she's a good neighbor and your best friend—and how she sometimes makes me a banana cream pie? And I should be ashamed?"

Gracie slipped out of her apron. "You know all that."

"Sure do!" He plunged his hands into suds. "But sometimes us old codgers need to be reminded."

She took a moment she truly couldn't spare to drop a kiss onto his weathered cheek.

12

"IS IT TRUE, GRACIE?" greeted her as she entered the sanctuary. She moved forward slowly. For a wonder, Barb wasn't rapping her baton—and it was three minutes past starting time! The question was repeated in the choir's full range of voices, clamoring for news.

"Is it? Is it really true that the money's been stolen?"

"Not stolen!" Gracie said, though a small nagging doubt nibbled at the back of her mind. "No!" she said firmly. "Not stolen at all. Simply mislaid."

"How could anyone mislay—" Tish began.

"All that money?" finished Tyne. Then understanding broke over their faces, and they said in unison, "But this is Nancyalma!"

"Exactly!" Estelle snorted. "And where is she this evening again?"

Gracie, suspecting that Nancyalma was still praying desperately for the strength to tackle the chaos around her, said nothing.

Amy said gently, "She may be getting ready for her yard sale," and a chorus of protest flared.

"A yard sale?"

"When we're waiting for her to produce the money she took—money earmarked for Patsy?"

"Why hasn't anyone called Herb Bower?"

"The yard sale's a way to force her to clear all that stuff! It's just what she needs, and then the money will come to light."

Barb tapped her baton. "That's right. Nancyalma's our friend! She wouldn't take a toothpick without asking first! Now let's get to work. There are a few tricky spots in this anthem, remember. Amy, you'll take the solo on page three, and again in the reprise, where you and Rick have a lovely duet."

Amy nodded.

Gracie flicked a glance toward Estelle, who reacted only slightly.

"And, Estelle, there's a lovely obligato on pages four and five. Could you—"

"Of course I *could*," Estelle emphasized, as though "would" might be questionable. "I'm a trained singer, remember."

A stifled groan rippled through the group.

Barb's baton tapped a brisk tattoo. "Let's do it, then, folks!"

"Lovely," Gracie whispered to Amy as they turned in their sheet music and descended from the choir loft.

"Thank you." Amy's blue eyes were wide, and her forehead tried unsuccessfully to form frown lines. "Gracie—you don't seem worried. About the money. Are you?"

"Of course not!" She sent up a quick prayer for forgiveness, since she suspected a half-truth was first cousin to an outright lie. "We're going to find it. I'm helping Nancyalma tomorrow again. Her brother's promised to carry some heavy furniture from the attic. She's convinced—and so am I—that as we get things ready for the yard sale, that money will show up."

Oops. Did two half-truths equal a full lie?

Sunday morning, the anthem went beautifully. Only a few of the children covered their ears during the obligato, though one infant woke, cried and had to be taken from the sanctuary.

Gracie offered Amy a lift to Abe's Deli, since Pastor Paul had run a few minutes late. Amy waited until they'd dropped Uncle Miltie off at home before asking, "You didn't find anything again yesterday, did you?"

Gracie reached to pat Amy's arm. "No, dear, but we did come across some rather exciting discoveries! An antique horsehair hat box in better-than-average condition . . . a brass spittoon, if you can imagine! When it's cleaned up, it should bring a nice price!"

Amy made a face. "You mean there was still . . . tobacco stuff in it?"

Gracie laughed. Even Nancyalma wasn't such a poor housekeeper. At least Gracie didn't think so. "I meant—as soon as the brass is polished. It's really a nicely shaped object—if we can forget its purpose. There's not a dent in it."

"I guess nobody can spit tobacco juice that hard!"

"I guess."

While Gracie parked Fannie Mae, Amy hurried inside.

At Rocky's little black sedan, she stopped to pet his two dogs whose heads protruded from the sun roof. They greeted Gracie with eager barks. "No treats today," she said, rubbing their muzzles. "Maybe after lunch!"

Inside Abe's, she moved carefully among the red formica and polished aluminum tables and sat opposite Rocky in their usual booth.

"How was church?" he asked.

"Lovely." If he'd go for himself, he'd know, she thought wistfully. "Amy sang a solo—lovely as usual, and she and Rick did a wonderful duet. I could have listened all day. Oh—and Estelle had an obligato that soared halfway to the stratosphere."

"I think I heard part of it." Rocky poured iced tea into their glasses. "I happened to be passing that way, and at first

I wondered what a screech-owl was doing out in the day-time." He grinned.

"Rocky!" But it was difficult for her to keep her face straight. "And we're not being fair. The deadly diva really does have an amazing range."

"Uh-huh."

Before she could defend Estelle further—and salve her own conscience—Gracie looked up to return Abe's greeting.

"Feeling better?"

"I'm too stubborn to stay sick for long." He slid into one of the remaining chairs. "And what about the mysterious missing money? Everyone's whispering about it."

"Still mysteriously missing."

"But you have faith that it will turn up?"

Gracie hesitated. "Let's say that I have faith that God knows where it is."

"A safe bet, I'd say. But do you have faith that God will lead you to it?"

Rocky said dryly, "If so, He's certainly taking the long scenic route!"

Abe chuckled comfortably. "He has been known to do that. Forty years in the wilderness, for example, is quite a hike!"

"Even for Gracie, here," Rocky teased.

"They must have been going in circles much of the time," Abe continued. "I have been there, and the whole area could easily get lost on our Great Plains."

"They needed time to grow up." Gracie sipped her tea. The ice cubes rattled merrily against cool glass. "I've always thought they were aptly named 'the *children* of Israel.' They certainly exemplified childishness—whining, complaining, rebelling, squabbling."

"As adults—not only in Israel—still do!" Abe said. "Of course none of *us* exhibit such flaws."

"Well . . ." Rocky tapped his chin in mock-contemplation. "At least *I* don't!"

"*Hmmm.*" Abe smiled broadly.

"No comment," Gracie contributed.

Amy set a napkin-covered basket in the center of their table. Rocky sniffed deeply. "*Ahhh.*"

"Fresh from the oven," Abe said proudly.

"Me first!" Rocky lifted the corner of the napkin and extracted an onion roll. "As I said, no childish characteristics here!"

They laughed companionably together.

Gracie took a roll—so warm she had to juggle it to keep from searing her fingertips—broke it and slathered it with butter that melted on contact. "Sophie?" she asked.

Abe nodded. "I have to hand it to her, she's a chip off the old brother!" He cleared his throat. "The money," he reminded Gracie. "What if it's never found?"

Gracie met his gaze squarely. "We'd have to raise more, I suppose."

"I think Abe may mean—" Rocky spoke between bites of a second roll, "—will charges be pressed?"

Gracie nearly choked. "Charge Nancyalma?"

"Not Nancyalma."

"Oh." So Rocky believed as Uncle Miltie did, that Monty Montgomery had taken it.

Abe leaned forward on his elbows. "There once was a man—"

"In a far country?" Rocky asked.

Abe chuckled. "You know the story? So soon?"

"It's just that I know the storyteller," Rocky answered.

Gracie sent Abe an encouraging glance.

"—in a distant country," Abe continued, but not for long.

"Isn't 'distant' just a synonym for 'far'?"

"Rocky!" chided Gracie.

But the story was interrupted once again by Amy, ready to take their orders. Its completion would have to wait for another day.

That afternoon, Pastor Paul stopped by. While Gracie gardened, Pastor Paul and Uncle Miltie played a cutthroat game of checkers.

"I've already beat him twice," Pastor Paul said, "so do I get a slice of that lemon pound cake I see over there?"

Uncle Miltie grumbled. "How do you like that? Taking food out of the mouths of his parishioners?"

While the men indulged, Gracie and Gooseberry walked outside into soft Indian summer sunshine. The flowerbeds were glorious. It was what Gracie called a sleepy day—still, warm, and quiet. She had nodded off in a lawnchair, Gooseberry on her lap, when she woke to the sound of a car door and looked up to see Blaise Bloomfield hurrying toward her, her full cotton skirt swishing as she walked.

She paused, propped her hands on her hips and said, "So that's what Gracie Lynn Parks looks like when she stops bustling!"

Gracie yawned pleasurably. "Look who's talking! You're like a hummingbird, darting from one place to another." She indicated another lawnchair. "Please. Sit down."

"I can stay only a minute. Actually—"

"King me!" Uncle Miltie crowed loudly. "Now I've got you!"

Pastor Paul's laughing answer was muted—but Blaise had obviously recognized his voice. Her face colored attractively. Her hands fussed in her lap. "I didn't know—" she began, then, rising quickly, "I'd better come back another time."

"Sit," Gracie said. "At the moment he and Uncle Miltie don't know that a world exists beyond the checkerboard."

"I don't want him to think I'm . . . stalking him!" Blaise said wretchedly.

"Why ever would he think that, dear child?"

"Because I . . . we . . . keep turning up at the same places."

Gracie pointed out, "In a town as small as Willow Bend, that's hard to avoid, don't you think?"

"Oh, I suppose, but—" Her pretty face clouded. Her hands twisted a piece of her skirt fabric. "Oh, Gracie! I'm so confused!"

Gracie determined that this was a good time simply to listen.

"He's such a great guy." Blaise looked to her hostess as though for confirmation.

Gracie nodded dutifully.

"And there are times I think—I really think I might—I mean, there are times I think being a minister's wife would be . . ." She broke off, then finished miserably, "I shouldn't even be thinking this, much less saying it."

"Why not, dear? Why shouldn't you be as human as the rest of humanity? You're attracted to him, as I'm certain he is to you—"

"That's just it," Blaise interrupted in an intense whisper. "I'm not sure at all that he is. Interested in me." Turning away, she dabbed at her eyes.

"Well, if he isn't," Gracie said firmly, "then he not only needs his eyes examined, he needs a heart transplant."

Blaise smiled tremulously.

For a moment, neither said a word. Gracie searched the silence for sounds not associated with a fierce checker competition and caught a whir of insects, a sleepy midday murmur of birds, a distant engine, a nearby sniffle.

Then Blaise cleared her throat. "Gracie? Is it that uncertain for you?"

Gracie smiled dreamily, "Elmo and I . . ."

"But I don't mean you and Elmo! I've heard what a wonderful marriage that was. But you and Mr. Gravino—"

"Rocky?" It was Gracie's turn to blush. "But Rocky and I—I mean, neither of us has ever said—"

"Exactly," Blaise said. "That's exactly where Paul and I stand."

13

THURSDAY, MIDAFTERNOON, Gracie and Uncle Miltie reported together to Nancyalma's house to help her organize for the yard sale.

Montgomery X. Montgomery stood outside looking more the disgruntled lumberjack than the suave auctioneer. He wore a red-checked flannel shirt, ankle-high boots, and at least three days' growth of stubble.

"Good day, Monty," Uncle Miltie said pleasantly, as if he liked and trusted the man.

"Depends," Monty grunted. "Any day that promises dust and splinters with a side order of spiders sounds anything *but* good to me."

"Gracie, dear!" Apron flapping, Nancyalma rushed to offer a hug. "And George Morgan!" He stepped back—fearing a hug of his own, Gracie was sure. "How sweet of you to come, too!"

"Marge is on her way," Gracie said. "She and Uncle Miltie have both had a great deal of experience with yard sales."

"Back in Ohio," Uncle Miltie said. "Doris, my dear wife, liked to have one spring and fall."

"Then you'll be a great help! This will be my first."

Uncle Miltie said—disingenuously, Gracie felt—"Then you should have a lot of good stuff."

"Oh, yes! But we want to do it right! What would you suggest?"

"What have you done so far?" When she didn't answer at once, he added, "Signs?"

"Fluorescent orange. Monty will place them at street corners."

"You have your address on each one? And arrows?"

"You may think they should be larger. When you're driving—"

"Doris hated that!" Uncle Miltie interrupted. "People squinting at signs . . . veering all over the street . . . missing stop signs."

"We'll make the lettering and arrows really huge!"

A young voice spoke from the edge of the lawn. "I can do that, Mrs. Smith!" Patsy forced her walker to a faster pace. "My printing's good!"

"No school today, Patsy darling?" Uncle Miltie reached to muss her hair.

"Teachers' meeting, Mr. Morgan. Tomorrow, too." She hugged herself. "I can't wait! Can I help Saturday, Mrs. Smith? I'll do anything you want!"

"Of course, dear," Nancyalma said.

Gracie wondered if she even realized that Patsy was there.

"Oh, Gracie! Will we ever—do you think—be ready? Maybe it would have been wiser to wait for another weekend. But now it's been advertised—"

"Oh?" Uncle Miltie perked up.

"Just in the weekly shoppers—places like that."

He nodded approval. "Doris said those were the best."

"Oh. Good." Nancyalma sighed. "So I've done one thing right!"

"At least," Patsy pointed out. "You already have your stuff all together."

"Well...."

"All in the same house," Montgomery muttered. "And that's the whole problem."

"Oh, Monty," his sister sighed. "You know you'll enjoy it! Just think how much fun you had at the auction!"

"That's true! But that was like being on stage. This is more like cleaning up after the circus." He stalked off.

Nancyalma sighed again, deeply. "He's a good person, really. But he does have moods, sometimes. I know it has to be hard for him, staying here with me. He's such a perfectionist. It's no wonder he's frustrated."

Uncle Miltie said mildly, "You're doing him a favor, taking him in."

"Oh, George, I truly don't know. When he got here, he had to walk sideways to get to his bed. Until he tossed everything out of his room."

Hmmm, Gracie thought, that explains something.

"Still, you do give him a bed. And food, I presume."

She shrugged. "Well, Monty has so many likes and dislikes—no cheap coffees or soups. And the leanest cuts of meat. And only the very freshest vegetables. I've been getting them at farm markets. Monty says—and he's right, of course—you never know how long things have been lying in grocery stores—or even where they were raised. How they were harvested."

"Looks to me," Uncle Miltie told her, "like his perfectionism is making things pretty hard for you! And expensive, too."

"Uncle Miltie." Gracie laid a cautionary hand on his arm.

Nancyalma looked more distressed, even, than usual. "Poor, poor Monty! No one truly understands him!"

Or perhaps, thought Gracie—waving at Marge, who was just emerging from her car—we understand him far too well. . . . But she said, "What do we do first, boss?"

Nancyalma fluttered her hands and looked toward Uncle Miltie.

His chest expanded by at least a full two inches. "I'd suggest we gather everything out here—grouping it. We could make tables if you have some old doors and saw-horses? Or improvise. We have some at home, don't we, Gracie?" Without pausing for an answer—or even, it seemed, for breath—he continued, "And pricing. Nothing made Doris as furious as looking for a price—and not finding one!"

"Then let's get started! I wonder where Monty went!"

"As far from meaningful work as possible," Uncle Miltie whispered in Gracie's ear.

And while she shushed him, she thought he was probably right.

Soon, the lawn was crowded with more or less organized groupings: canisters and cooking pots; pottery pitchers and glass bowls; floor lamps and umbrella stands; vases of every size, shape and color; albums of stamps and coins and photos; fingerless gloves and embroidered dresser scarves no one seemed to use these days.

"Antique dealers will commit mayhem for some of these." Marge spread out a large pale green doily with a pineapple pattern.

"Maybe I shouldn't let them go?"

"Mrs. Smi-i-ith," Patsy sang out.

"I know. I know, dear. Hanging on to things has always been my downfall." She sighed. "I remember my great-grandmother crocheting—but with heavy yarn and a magni-fying lamp, at the last."

Patsy fingered the delicate doily. "Did she make this?"

Marge said, "When you arrive at a price, I'd love to buy some for the boutique."

Nancyalma turned away. "It doesn't matter," she said. "It truly doesn't." She straightened. "Marge—you decide which ones you want. A dollar apiece, or make me an offer. Fair enough?" She walked stiffly toward the house.

"I feel terrible." Marge couldn't seem to take her eyes from the lovely pieces. "I'll pay her more, of course, but this has to make her sad—"

"And desperate," Gracie reminded her.

"They take up practically no space!"

"Neither does a snowflake," Uncle Miltie said crisply, "but put enough of them together and they can bury you."

"I suppose—"

"Take them." Gracie reached for a plastic bag. "You're doing her a favor. Believe me."

Emerging with an ornate tasseled lampshade, Nancyalma apologized, "I never even thought about a snack for us."

As if on cue, Montgomery appeared, yawning. "I'm hungry."

Nancyalma reminded him, "We've been working!"

Gracie suggested calling Abe. "Have him get some muffins ready. Monty, you could pick them up, couldn't you?"

"Sorry," he said, and wandered off.

Surveying her grubby apron and slacks, Nancyalma spread her grimy hands.

"We're all too dirty to go," Uncle Miltie agreed. "Maybe Abe would do us a favor and deliver."

"What a great idea!" Clapping him on the back, Gracie went for the phone. "I'll make the call, if you like."

Nancyalma sank gratefully to the grass. "Please," she said.

They ate in silence, except for various murmurs of approval. Patsy was the first to speak intelligibly. "Thank you, thank you, Mr. Wasserman!" She clumped to him, and he hugged her, walker and all. "That's the most scrumptious muffin I ever tasted!"

Abe chuckled. "For that *I* thank *you*, my dear Miss Clayton. It's nice to be appreciated."

The sorting and carrying resumed. But they had slowed down. Uncle Miltie expressed Gracie's thoughts when he said, "Good food defeats the will to work!"

And yet they accomplished wonders befeore they broke off for the day. Before they left Nancyalma alone, perhaps half of the items for Saturday's yard sale were priced, set out and protected with an assortment of tarps. On Friday the task would be manageable. Unfortunately, they were no closer than before to finding the missing money.

Nor had Gracie seen any evidence to support her theory that this was the original home of the N.A.M.S. wax carvings.

After a good stint on Friday, finishing up, Uncle Miltie went home for what he termed "quality time" with Gooseberry—

which surely, Gracie thought, meant them taking a nap together, either in the hammock or on the couch.

Gracie decided to swing by Marge's shop.

Nancyalma seemed reluctant to let her go. "I just can't tell you," she said for at least the tenth time, "how very much I appreciate all my friends have done for me!"

Gracie repeated the answer she herself was growing tired of hearing. "That's what friends are for."

Nancyalma sighed. "I know that's what they say—but there are friends . . . and there are *friends!* You're blue-ribbon all the way, Gracie Lynn Parks!"

After walking less than half of the few blocks to the shop, Gracie suddenly realized how tired she was.

It's strange, isn't it, she asked the Lord, *how the energy seems inexhaustible as long as the push is on . . . and then there doesn't seem to be a drop of adrenalin left?*

She veered to one side and slumped on a park bench. A squirrel skittered down the bole of an oak tree, surveyed her for a moment or two, and—apparently pronouncing her harmless—approached, mere inches at a time.

"No handouts today," she said softly. "Sorry."

Apparently taking her tone as invitation, he moved closer. His swishing tail brushed her ankle, and she found herself wishing that she, too, had gone home to take a nap beside Gooseberry.

The fearless squirrel hopped to the park bench and nosed

Gracie's pocket. Obviously, he had regular meal-providers.

But he flashed away as Herb Bowers' official car squealed to a stop. "Want a lift, Gracie? You look pretty bushed!"

"When Herb had to help you out of the car," Marge said—half in teasing, half in concern—"I thought maybe you'd been arrested."

"For loitering?" Gracie leaned back in an adjustable chair near the store's front window.

"Would you like an afghan?"

"Just tea, if you have it. I don't know what's wrong with me."

"What's wrong with you," Marge declared, clacking cups and spoons, "is that you're older than you think you are, and you're wearing yourself out. Burning the candle at both ends, and trying for the middle. And it's mostly for other people, who surely don't appreciate you half enough!" She poured tea and brought Gracie's cup to her.

"Thanks." She accepted the steaming brew gratefully. "And you're wrong, Marge. Folks here in Willow Bend are extremely appreciative."

"*Hmmm.* Some are, some aren't."

Gracie felt strength flowing through her. Ah, the power of the tea leaf! "Name one who isn't," she challenged.

"Barry Benton." Marge spoke without hesitation and with a great deal of venom.

Gracie drained her cup. "What's the boy done now?"

"Plenty." Marge reached for her cup. "Refill?"

"Please." She waited for the latest Barry bulletin.

"Last night. If you'd come in the back way, you'd have seen the shop window. Or where the window used to be."

Gracie smiled. "Barry stole your window?"

"Better if he had. It took me an hour to clean up the glass. It was everywhere! In boxes of clothing—winter things that didn't go in the spring sale. Thought I'd give them another chance. In a bushel basket of yarn. I'll never get all the shards out! Anyone who buys a skein will leave a few bloody stitches, I'm afraid!"

"And you're certain it was Barry."

"Exhibit A." She held up a ball. "Autographed by Daryl Strawberry, no less."

"And Barry should be grateful because—" She waited.

"Because I called to say I wouldn't press charges if he replaced the glass. And cleaned up the mess, of course." She sniffed and set down her cup with a clatter.

"He laughed. Said he'd been doing his homework at the time. Ha! How did he know what time?"

Gracie was definitely feeling stronger. She swung her legs over the side of the chair. "What did he say about the ball?"

"Just that I'd better give it back, or he'd sue me." She snorted. "Said it had been stolen! Can you imagine? But . . . to change the subject, let me show you my latest acquisition! Besides Nancyalma's doilies."

Those, Gracie noticed, Marge had already displayed artistically in one of the glass showcases.

"Nancyalma will be so pleased!"

"And Uncle Miltie? What about him?"

Gracie inhaled sharply. How had she missed it before? On an antique walnut piano bench, polished to a sheen, Elmo's / Uncle Miltie's carved eagle rested in state—its low marble pedestal swathed in gold satin.

Gracie caught Marge in an impromptu hug. "Pleased?" she asked. "He'll say that's one in the eye for Tyrone Sanders!"

GREAT DAY FOR A YARD SALE!" Uncle Miltie declared as he entered the kitchen Saturday morning. "A little cool now, maybe—but better cool than sizzling enough to melt the fillings in your teeth. When do we report for action?"

"As soon as possible."

"No praise-walk this morning?"

Gracie found teabags. "I'll do my praising on the run today."

"Works for me!" He yawned. "Want me to scramble eggs?"

"I was thinking waffles."

"Even better! Your special walnut-flavored ones?"

"If that's what you want."

"You know it! I'll get butter and syrup. Why don't we just use Styrofoam plates? Save time."

Gracie raised an eyebrow. "You deserve real dinnerware, Uncle Miltie. I can't imagine Aunt Doris setting anything less before you." She plugged in the waffle iron. "Nor will I."

"Just because she spoiled me—"

"I'll continue the tradition."

They were silent for a moment, as the iron heated, silverware clicked, and orange juice splashed into glasses.

When Uncle Miltie spoke again, his voice sounded clogged. "Have I told you lately how very much I appreciate you?"

She smiled fondly in his direction. "Not since dinnertime yesterday."

"Well, consider it said again." He went to the screen door, through which Gooseberry could be seen stalking a butterfly in the dew-damp grass.

🐇

When they arrived at her house, Nancyalma was in what Gracie's grandmother would have called "a swivet." She alternately paced, clapped both hands to her head, gazed heavenward in appeal, went to one table or another—picking up items and setting them down only centimeters from where they'd rested before.

Patsy followed her as best she could with her walker. "Please, Mrs. Smith! You're going to have a heart attack, and I don't know CPR!" Marilyn Clayton, Patsy's mother, was off in a corner, tidying a welter of flower pots and urns.

"Oh dear, oh dear, oh dear, oh dear," Nancyalma chanted— apparently oblivious to Patsy's concern . . . and of how difficult it was for the child to follow the erratic choreography of her pacing.

"Look, Mrs. Smith!" Patsy caught her arm in passing, and nearly lost her balance. "They're here—Mrs. Parks and Mr. Morgan! Now everything has to be all right!" She came clumping over to them, looking up into Gracie's face. "I'm really worried." She swallowed hard. "Do you know CPR?"

"I might." Uncle Miltie leaned his own walker against the bole of a maple tree. He hadn't needed it much recently but for such a long day he was better off prepared. "Only thing is, Patsy, I don't have the paddles."

"Paddles?" Patsy's face screwed up in confusion.

"Yes, paddles. Though there's pingpong equipment over there. That might work if we can get the juice to them."

"Juice?"

"Uncle Miltie. . . ." Gracie murmured.

"Electricity. Then I hold them together and make sure everybody's clear—"

"That's not CPR!"

"Close enough! Tell you what, young lady, go get those pingpong paddles and let me practice on you!" He lunged at her, and she collapsed in giggles on the grass.

"You're silly. Isn't he, Mrs. Parks? Silly?"

Gracie nodded. "And he gets worse every day. But we love him anyway, don't we?"

Patsy had lost her worried look. And Nancyalma, while still flitting from one spot to another, seemed not quite so frantic. Gracie waved a greeting to Marilyn Clayton.

Then she walked over to Nancyalma. "Everything looks fine!"

Nancyalma wrung her hands. "What if nobody comes? I want the money I take in to go to Patsy's medical fund, as well."

"They will come."

"But if they don't?"

"Then there are a lot of charity groups that will be very happy to take these lovely things off your hands."

"That's true."

Gracie asked, "Will Monty be helping out today?"

"Monty? Oh. No. He's inside, searching closets and under beds."

Searching for the auction money, Gracie surmised. She threw Uncle Miltie a quick glance to see if he'd heard.

He obviously had. Snatching his walker from its resting place he said, "Tell you what, Nancyalma, I'll go help him. You women are better at this yard sale stuff, anyway. We men are better at the treasure hunts."

When he was gone, Nancyalma sighed. "I hope Monty doesn't bite his head off. He's been a perfect bear, ever since—" She caught Gracie's arm. "They're here! Our very first customers!"

And that was merely the beginning.

Cordelia Fountain arrived with the first three browsers.

She wore her period costume, carried a folded pale blue parasol and a drawstring jet-beaded bag. The other gloved hand juggled what could only be leaflets. What now? Gracie wondered, but curiosity was soon satisfied.

Handing Gracie one of the folded sheets, Cordelia whispered, "Isn't this exciting, Gracie? I should thank Nancyalma for providing such a convenient opportunity for me to do some promotion."

"That would be nice."

Cordelia frowned. "Pardon?"

"If you thank her. It would be nice."

Cordelia didn't quite agree. "She should thank me! How many yard sales get this extra historic atmosphere? It's all mostly junk and stuff until you're helped to view it in context." She swished away, her full skirts brushing the various tables laden with Nancyalma's treasures.

"Look at this." One shopper stroked a highly varnished magazine rack shaped somewhat like a swan. Another checked a carnival-glass pitcher for cracks and chips, while the third rummaged through stacks of books, emerging at length with a yip of triumph. She held up a *Daily Guideposts* devotional book of several years earlier.

As other cars parked nearby and eager people—chattering and laughing—rushed to join the fray, Gracie watched, fascinated from the umbrella-shaded table where she would total purchases and receive receipts. *It never fails to amaze me,* she thought—between customers—*what people will buy. It must amuse You, too, Lord, that these creatures You created find such pleasure in rummaging through someone else's castoffs.*

And yet she had done it herself. Many times. In memory she could catalog those "found treasures" she had taken home from yard sales and flea markets in triumph. *After all,* she told the Lord, *the cast-off you buy was perhaps a prized heirloom in another time. And if it needs a bit of shining to show its true beauty, so much the better.*

A strange thought hit her. *Lord, we're like that to You, aren't we? You find us . . . treasure us . . . dust us off and call us Your own.*

Someone cleared his throat. "Sorry to wake you up, young lady."

Rocky! Her cheeks felt inflamed.

"I was—"

"Daydreaming," he said, chuckling. "I recognize the look. I've seen it before."

"Actually," she said, "I was . . . talking to God." She never knew how he might react when she spoke of her faith. Often his lips tightened, showing that he was closing himself off from involvement. This time he simply asked, "And what did the two of you say?"

"Oh, this and that." She grinned. "We were discussing the philosophy of junk. You know, the tarnished treasure sort. And also the beautiful day."

"I suppose He took credit for that."

"He didn't have to. I knew."

He shifted position, and she felt it was time to change the subject. "You found something you want to buy?"

He sank to a nearby folding chair and lowered his voice. "This . . . accumulation is remarkable!" He laid one of Cordelia's leaflets under the table. "How did it all fit in that house? And talk about eclectic style—" He leaned back and crossed his legs, but the chair stood on uneven ground, and he quickly unfolded for balance. "Maybe I should do a feature."

"On Nancyalma?"

"On the reselling of one's possessions in such a strangely intimate way. What draws someone to one thing and not another? Why deliberately go for baubles over pearls? The whole yard sale phenomenon is so uniquely American!"

"We all follow our noses to that object that calls out, 'Buy me! Buy me!'" Gracie laughed.

"Art Deco turns some people on, while others want Shaker." For a moment Rocky simply watched the activity, as did Gracie. "A dress one woman discards makes another feel special."

One browser fingered a filigree picture frame holding a photo of a child. The picture was of no one Nancyalma knew, Gracie intuited—just a frame she had bought, never replacing the anonymous photo with a personal one. However, the woman ran her fingertips across the glass, as though caressing the child. Then she set it down gently. As she turned away, Gracie was sure she saw the glint of tears.

"She lost a child of her own," Gracie guessed. "Either by death or estrangement."

Rocky looked at her with what seemed a mixture of amusement and respect.

Dear Lord, she thought quickly—not wanting to ignore Rocky, but needing to say something while compassion swelled her heart. *Dear Lord, bless that woman. And heal her. If her child died, help her to realize that he or she is with You. But if a child has grown estranged, then please, Lord, while there is time, let there be reconciliation—*

"Got an idea," Rocky said, a light of challenge in his eyes and in the tilt of his head. "I'll go pick out six things you would choose, and if I'm right, you explain why."

Before Gracie could respond, a young woman asked, "Do I pay here?" Three children of stairstep heights waited patiently with her. One held a book on dinosaurs. The second offered a small box of colorful pebbles. And the youngest, a little girl, wore a necklace fashioned of three long strands of strung seashells separated by fluorescent pink beads.

"For Mommy," she whispered in Gracie's ear. "Think she'll like it?" She touched one of the shells to her cheek.

Gracie smiled reassurance, certain that her mother would show delight merely to please the child—though where could she wear such a gaudy trinket?

"Your family might be interested in this!" Cordelia fluttered over with her leaflets. She crouched down. "Do you like history?" she asked the oldest.

"What's his-try, Mama?"

Cordelia rushed in. "It's about all the things that have happened to people who lived long, long ago! I've copied it so more people can read it."

The kids looked skeptical.

Cordelia remained determined. "Let me read you something here, dear. This precious girl is writing about her cat. 'Fluffy chased a chipmunk today. She looked really puzzled when the chipmunk went into a hole high up in the tree. If cats can frown, she did. Then she scooted down, and I called her to me. I was glad the chipmunk got away. I don't want to think about anyone hurting someone else—even animals.' There. Wouldn't you like to know more about the little girl?"

"I want to meet the cat!" The tiny girl tugged at her seashell necklace.

"If it lived that long ago, it'd be dead, silly!" Her brother made a face at her.

"Don't tease her," the mother scolded softly, but the little girl's lower lip was trembling. "Come, kids, pay for your things, and we'll go have Sno-cones. How would that be?"

"Yeah! I want raspberry!"

"You always get raspberry!"

137

"Sooooooo?"

As they left, Cordelia sighed loudly. "No curiosity!" she declared. "What's the world coming to?"

"They're children, dear!"

"The mother isn't." Cordelia was not to be budged.

Gracie said mildly, "The mother has her hands too full of the present just now to be too concerned with history."

"I'll find someone who'll appreciate my efforts to educate them," Cordelia vowed as she swished away, clutching her leaflets.

"How much is this?" a lilting voice asked.

"Everything should be marked," Gracie replied automatically. Then she looked up.

It was Blaise Bloomfield.

She wore a long denim jumper over a short-sleeved white T-shirt, and looked cool and crisp as usual.

"I can't find a price." Blaise held a wax carving of a parrot. With a wick.

Gracie frowned. "Are the letters NAMS carved into the base?

Blaise looked. "How did you know?"

Gracie said, "I doubt it's for sale."

"I found it—" Blaise gestured toward a nearby table.

"I think it may have been left there by accident. Ask Nancyalma."

"Did I just hear my name?" The homeowner herself wandered over. Gracie was delighted to see her now looking relaxed. "Oh, Gracie, I'm enjoying myself so much! Aren't you?"

Gracie assured her that she was, indeed. She was about to mention the carving when Nancyalma emitted a glad little cry.

"Oh! Isn't that sweet! Where did you ever find it, Blaise?"

Blaise threw Nancyalma a startled look. "Over by the pillow cases. . . ."

"How well done it is!" Nancyalma turned it in her hands. Then her glance moved to Gracie. "Who do you suppose— And why—?"

Blaise tilted her head. "Then you were right, Gracie? It's not for sale?"

Nancyalma held it to her breast. "Oh, no," she said huskily. "I'd never sell this."

"So," Blaise asked, when Nancyalma had carried her new trophy proudly away, "how is it going? Really."

"The . . . yard sale seems quite a success."

"And . . . ?"

"The money? Not yet."

Both turned to look after Nancyalma.

"That poor woman." Blaise shuddered. "I can't imagine the tension she must feel!"

Of course! That's the reason for the carvings, isn't it, Lord? The artist is trying to comfort anyone sick or upset. The Searfosses in the hospital, Amy—limping, Abe sick with flu, Nancyalma—but I'd thought she might be the carver, Lord! And she can't be! Not unless she's a better actress than I'd ever thought she could be!

139

THERE WAS LITTLE TIME to ponder this unexpected turn of events. A flurry of buyers eager to pay for their finds had crowded around Gracie's table.

Barb Jennings, predictably, had chosen plaster busts of Bach, Brahms and Beethoven. "Inspiration," she confided. "How can my playing not improve with them looking on?"

"There's nothing wrong with your playing now," Gracie assured her. She herself would have found the presence of three such masters intimidating. She carefully wrapped each of the musical gentlemen in newspaper, then placed them in a plastic bag.

Barb's other items were more of a surprise: a rusted pair of pruning shears for rosebushes ("I may plant some next year. I've always loved roses, but I have two black thumbs."); a tarnished cream pitcher and lidless sugar bowl ("My great-aunt had one just like this. Won't it look lovely with a little silver polish?").

Rather, a *lot* of silver polish, Gracie thought, but said, "They're shaped beautifully. Anything else?"

Barb then offered a battered Scrabble board with a limited collection of tiles. "So I'll always have words," she laughed, but didn't actually explain what use there could be in an incomplete set, or why she had made this particular selection.

Marge's various purchases also offered some surprises. Except for Uncle Miltie—and Gooseberry, of course—Gracie was closer to Marge than anyone else in the world. She would never have expected Marge—who prized herself on her well-groomed hands—to buy oily slip-joint pliers or an unopened package of jigsaw blades. Or that Marge—whose hair was perfectly coiffed even when grocery shopping—would invest in floppy, frayed sunhats and woolen caps.

"Isn't this precious?" Marge held up a silk kimono, riotous with magentas and blues. "It doesn't look the least bit like Nancyalma, does it?" She giggled, whispering wickedly, "Maybe it was Monty's!"

"It will look smashing on you, though."

"And this." Being careful of her nails, Marge hoisted a glass-imbedded stepping stone to Gracie's table. "I've always wanted one for near the birdbath."

Gracie smiled. The only birds to enjoy the lovely stone

would have to be those interested in dry-cleaning. She hadn't seen water in Marge's birdbath since the April rains.

"Would you mind keeping some of this stuff until later? I need to look around some more."

Gracie helped her friend tuck everything but the kimono beneath the table.

Next in line was Amy Cantrell. "What do you think?" She held a three-stranded choker of silver geometric shapes and sapphire-blue glass beads.

"It brings out the color of your eyes."

"Or this?"

A turquoise pendant with a hole just off-center hung on a long black cord.

"Beautiful, too."

"Or this?" It was a chunky necklace—uneven shapes of hardened clay, a few silver-colored springs and—"What are those?" Gracie asked.

Amy giggled. "Can you believe it? Sliced seashells! Did you ever hear of such a thing?"

"Move it!" grumbled Barry Benton—clearly impatient with the amount of time Amy was taking.

Amy turned her thousand-watt smile on him. "Please, Barry, just a minute more? I need Gracie's advice."

Startled, he said, "Okay. But just a minute!"

"Which?" Amy asked earnestly.

"Why not all three?"

Handing them over, Amy giggled. "I was hoping you'd say that!"

Gracie had no problem determining Amy's reasons for choosing the jewelry. She was young, attractive and fond of unusual things.

But why on earth would she buy a cardboard box of canning jars, a non-functioning music-box and a battered corduroy cushion?

On the other hand, Barry's purchases were wholly predictable—baseballs, tennis balls, badminton birdies and a slingshot. "Not a single surfboard here," he grumbled, slamming his money to the table. If he had been anyone pleasant, Gracie would have asked him where the waves were running the highest in Willow Bend, Indiana.

But possibly he planned a move to California. Or was that too much to hope for? Twelve years old and a schoolboy still, he'd have the truant officer after him in a flash, if there still *were* truant officers.

As she took the next customer . . . and the next . . . Gracie wondered what luck Rocky would have in predicting her preferences.

There's no rhyme or reason, is there, Lord—to explain why we make the choices we do? And it's understandable, isn't it? Each of us is such a unique bundle of interests, experiences and memories.

"Next," Tish and Tyne sang, offering identical items: two battered dolls; two kaleidoscopes; two sets of wooden salad bowls; and two pairs of high-button boots.

Gracie hadn't seen Patsy, lurking nearby, until she'd recorded sales for three more shoppers.

The child wobbled over. "Are you lonesome, Mrs. Parks?"

"I am if you feel like a visit."

"I was helping. But I got sort of tired and sad."

"Sit here with me."

"But—Mr. Gravino—"

"—is shopping."

"For tools and things?" Patsy added, "There aren't many."

"He's shopping . . . for me."

"Oh. You gave him a shopping list?"

"Not . . . exactly. I don't have any idea what he'll choose."

Patsy squealed. "He's buying you *presents*? At a *yard sale*?"

"Not presents. Not even buying." She leaned closer, and Patsy did the same. Their heads nearly touched. Patsy's hair smelled like strawberries. "He's trying to predict what items I'd have picked."

Patsy considered that, a forefinger to pursed lips. "He won't be able to, will he? Men aren't very smart about what women like—are they?"

"Many aren't," Gracie began, then whispered, "He's coming!"

Giggling, Patsy bounced on her chair.

"So what do you two ladies find so amusing?" Rocky asked, guarding the contents of a large wicker basket.

"Would you have liked the basket, Mrs. Parks?"

Rocky interjected, "It's just to carry the things I selected."

"Though I might have," Gracie said. "I need an unusual planter for an arrangement of small philodendrons and ferns."

"Imagine that!" Rocky sorted among the items in the basket and extracted a lovely glass paperweight, colors swirling in an abstract flower design. "Even when I don't know I'm picking the right thing, I'm picking the right thing."

"You're phenomenal," Gracie said dryly.

But Patsy had eyes only for the paperweight. "*Ooooooh!*" she breathed, her eyes widening. "Oh, don't you love it?"

Gracie turned it to catch the light. "It is beautiful—but there was another I liked better. More blues and gr—"

"This one?" Rocky crowed. "Gotcha!"

"I don't know what I'd do with it!"

"It's a paperweight, Mrs. Parks," Patsy informed her. "You hold down paper with it."

Rocky tried to hide a smile.

"These are really for collectors. Uncle Miltie and I suggested a higher price—"

"Bought and paid for. Except the basket, and I'll take care of that." He handed the first paperweight to Patsy.

She hugged it close to her chest. "Mr. Gravino! You don't mean—"

145

"I do mean," he said, smiling. "And I hope you'll do what Gracie's going to do with hers—place it on a window sill to catch the morning sun."

Patsy was thrilled. Her little face split practically in half with pleasure. Gracie, afraid her chair might tilt under such exuberance, reached to steady it.

Patsy bounded out of it, clutched the paperweight in one hand and with the other tried to maneuver her walker. "I'm going to show—everybody! Thank you, Mr. Gravino! A lot!"

They watched for a moment, wincing each time she stumbled, breathing a sigh of relief when she came to a stop by Rick Harding and his family.

"At least someone gets excited by my gift-buying expertise."

Gracie said, "I can't believe you paid for all of this—before you knew."

"I knew," he said, "because I know you."

"No one knows anyone else that well."

"I do."

He looked so smug that Gracie couldn't resist saying, "Sounds like an acute attack of male arrogance, if you ask me."

"I didn't ask you. But I consider it a matter of faith in myself."

Gracie determined that she was going to hate—or at least pretend to—whatever he showed her next. But she couldn't help herself. It was an old recipe journal, with handwritten entries. Notations about how each recipe had come about made it even more precious. "I didn't see this. Yesterday, when we set up."

"Nancyalma said it wasn't out then. She stumbled across it just this morning."

"Oh, Rocky, this is lovely!"

"And insightful?" he urged.

"Even insightful! Thank you!"

"Told you I could do it!"

However, he turned out to be a little less lucky with his other choices. Gracie was unimpressed with the plastic soap dispenser in the shape of a tomato. And the gourd birdhouse. And the cushions with cats on them.

"I don't get it." Rocky shook his head.

"I prefer living creatures to representations of them. Cats, yes. Cat *things*, no."

"But I thought these were—"

"Exactly."

"Exactly what?"

"Exactly what I was saying before. That we can't predict what someone else—faced with such a smorgasbord—will choose."

"Well, I know if I'd bought all of Nancyalma's mystery paperbacks, you'd be happy with my choice. But I needed a greater challenge."

"Only if I hadn't read them would that have worked," Gracie corrected him. "And besides, they would only remind me of the mystery we're still facing."

It was mid-afternoon when Nancyalma walked unsteadily to Gracie's table and slumped into the chair Rocky had left only recently.

"Poor dear," Gracie said, "I should have traded off with you. You've been on your feet all day."

"I'm exhausted. I've never been so worn out! Gracie—"

Gracie waited.

"I know we said we'd look again for the choir money later today, with so much cleared away."

Gracie said, "What difference will another two days make? That's all right, dear." But Gracie was worried.

Obviously Montgomery and Uncle Miltie had made no progress.

As though following her train of thought, Nancyalma said, "Uncle Miltie's taking a nap over there. He tried looking around, to see what was left—I think he was particularly interested in a set of old *Popular Mechanics* from the 1950s. He seemed annoyed because, he said, everywhere he went he bumped into 'that woman.'"

"Marge?"

"Cordelia and her 'dratted leaflets.'"

Gracie laughed fondly. That was Uncle Miltie, without a doubt. "And Monty?" she asked.

"He seemed exhausted, too. I think he's gone up to his room to relax before dinner."

Or to continue the search without witnesses, Gracie thought.

"Which is exactly what I'm going to do, once everything's cleared." Nancyalma peered at the sky. "Don't you think it's going to rain, Gracie?" She sounded wistful.

Gracie glanced at her watch. "It's nearly five. People will be starting to think about dinner, settling down for the evening. We can begin packing up soon, so you rest here for now."

Nancyalma stood up. "We did well . . . don't you think? There won't be more than a couple of carloads to give to the charity thrift shop over in Mason City."

"Yes, my dear friend, you had a very successful first yard sale!"

And I think I'll put that plastic tomato back just in case someone else falls in love with it before we shut down, Gracie thought to herself.

16

IT WAS THE CHOIR PRACTICE for the final Sunday before Patsy's surgery. As usual, Barb raised her baton, sheet music rustled, and practice began on the dot.

> *For evening stars and cookie jars,*
> *we thank You, Lord!*
> *For kitchen stools and swimming pools,*
> *we thank You, Lord!*
> *For ice cream licks and candles' wicks,*
> *kangaroos and petting zoos,*
> *crickets' "cricks" and yo-yo tricks,*
> *we thank You,*
> *thank You,*
> *thank You, Lord!*

For cantaloupe and bubbly soap,
we thank You, Lord!
For boats with sails, and bunny tails,
we thank You, Lord!
For babies' sighs and butterflies,
raindrops' dances, second chances,
kite-filled skies and Easter dyes,
we thank You
thank You,
thank You, Lord!

For candy dishes, birthday wishes,
we thank You, Lord!
For puppies' barks and campfires' sparks,
we thank You, Lord!
For weeds that tumble, bees that bumble,
the camel's hump and frogs that jump,
thunder's grumble and skates that rumble,
we thank You,
thank You,
thank You, Lord!

Closing with a flurry of notes and one decisive chord, Barb leaned perilously back on her wobbly piano stool and asked, "Well?"

"Delightful!" Tish cooed.

Tyne clasped her hands. "Absolutely charming."

"Sweet." Nancyalma smiled broadly.

Gracie was delighted that Nancyalma had felt comfortable with attending choir practice again. "Nobody has even *mentioned* the missing money!" she had confided to Gracie. "Willow Bend people are so *loving.* And I haven't even told them yet how well the yard sale did!"

"Sweet!" sniffed Estelle. "Saccharine, rather! I feel as though—as though I should wear a pinafore and braids!"

"Would you?" teased Lester Twomley, and earned himself a glare.

"Hmmph!" Estelle snorted.

Barb stiffened. "It's Patsy's favorite song!"

"Exactly. And Patsy's a child. We're—at least we're *supposed* to be—adults!"

Gracie said gently, "Adults who want to comfort a dear young friend facing surgery. *Again.*"

Estelle's voice wobbled. "I'd just feel so . . . s-silly."

Gracie, suspecting that the glint in Estelle's eyes originated as much from tears as from stubbornness, touched the woman's elbow.

Estelle jerked away. "I suppose you approve, Gracie Lynn Parks!"

Gracie nodded. "In fact, I suggested it." *Am I wrong?* she asked the Lord. *It seemed such a right thing to do, to show Patsy how much we care. But if Estelle truly finds it embarrassing. . . .*

"There isn't a decent soprano phrase in the whole song!"

Estelle flared—and the choir, in harmony, breathed a long, informed *Ahhh!*

So it was Estelle's professional pride, rather than a sense of propriety, that was threatened.

Barb thumped a chord. "Then it's settled!" she decreed. "We'll do it! If anyone wants to stage a protest, feel free to fake laryngitis."

"Like Rick?" Amy giggled. "When he wanted to get out of auctioneering?"

Everyone—except Estelle—laughed.

Then, because Barb's gentle nature couldn't allow her to be authoritative for long, she added, "We'll sing it just after the children's message."

Estelle, already halfway up the aisle, paused only momentarily.

Sunday itself was dismal—one of those rainy days, Uncle Miltie predicted glumly, that was a harbinger of season's change. He hugged himself as though winter had already arrived.

"It's a perfect morning for cinnamon toast." Gracie patted his back on her way to the sink and hummed a few bars of "Oh, What a Beautiful Morning" as she sliced some home-made bread. When he remained in a grumpy slump, she asked gently, "Arthritis kicking up this morning?"

"You know me too well."

Gracie sat down and took his gnarled hands in hers. "Days like this sometimes depressed Elmo a bit, too. And he did hate to think of winter coming." She chuckled at the memory. "The Fourth of July, he'd say, 'Well, won't be long until the snow flies.' Of course he was joking."

"Maybe and maybe not. The boy had good sense!" He glared at her. "You know that you're my favorite person still in this world, barring none—and not too many on the other side could compete. But I've got to tell you—when you're cheerful on a day like this, it makes me think seriously about divorce." He managed a small smile. "That is, if an uncle can divorce a niece."

"Well, then—" She gave his hands a light squeeze and pushed back from the table. "How's this?" and as she measured and stirred, she hummed a one-toned funeral dirge.

She could hear him giving up the battle, succumbing to laughter. At last he pleaded, "Enough! Have mercy! You'll be the death of me yet, Gracie, girl," he declared, "one way or another!"

"Today," Pastor Paul said before beginning announcements, "we make our own sunshine!"

Gracie could hear rain pattering and sliding down the beautiful flow-green windows that always infused her thoughts with springlike buoyancy—whatever the weather outside. *Of course it's more than that,* she told the Lord as everyone rose for the Call to Worship. *It's You, being here with us. Of course You always are with Your flock—wherever we are—but here Your Eternal Hope lambs all experience You at the same time.*

It was like ice cream, she thought, remembering how, even as a child, she'd loved the dessert best when it was shared. That way she could absorb the appreciative *"Mmmms"* and lip-smackings of everyone, thus multiplying her own enjoyment.

Some might question the appropriateness of comparing God's love to ice cream. *But, Lord, Your love nourishes the soul—and ice cream is considered by some of us to be the perfect food. Both fill us to the brim with satisfaction and well-being. Both produce a joyful glow. Both are delicious in every way.*

Barb's baton rapped, and Gracie realized with some chagrin that it was already time for the anthem. She'd really have to stop monopolizing God during church!

Just now, the choir had a special song to sing for Patsy.

Gracie watched closely to see the child's reaction. Before the piano began tinkling the sprightly introduction, Patsy leaned against her mother, both of their expressions a bit strained. After a few bars, Patsy straightened, seeming intent. With the first phrase, a grin began, and by the middle of the first stanza, she was bouncing in the pew. *See that, Lord?* Gracie asked with a chink of her mind. *There was never any doubt it was the right choice!*

After church, Patsy was besieged with well-wishers. Even

Estelle—apparently suffering only slight psychological damage in the aftermath of the anthem—gathered her in a smothering hug.

"Dear child," she trilled, "I shall come visit you in hospital and sing you a lullaby!"

Others made no such dire promises—or threats—but if Patsy didn't feel thoroughly adored after the assault of hugs, kisses and pats, it wasn't for lack of everyone's efforts.

It's one of the things I love most about Eternal Hope, Lord— that we are a family. Your family.

Patsy was glowing when she caught up to Gracie in the parking lot. Although the rain had stopped, the clouds hung heavy, the air was cool, and puddles spotted the pavement. Hoping that Patsy's small walker wouldn't slip, Gracie slowed at its tap-tap-tap.

"Mrs. Parks! Mrs. Parks!"

Gracie turned, opening her arms.

"I feel all black and blue from hugs!" Patsy said, eyes sparkling. Nonetheless, she leaned into Gracie's embrace, her own arms scarcely reaching to Gracie's waist. "I loved the song! That was your idea, wasn't it, Mrs. Parks?"

Patsy's mother, breaking from a conversation with Marybeth Bower and Linda Cantrell, gathered both Gracie and Patsy into her arms. "You're a good friend, Gracie Parks," she said, her voice thick with emotion. "I don't think Willow Bend could get along without you."

Gracie felt herself blushing. "They'd do just fine," she murmured.

"No!" Patsy protested. "You're the goodest, Mrs. Parks!" She waved at Uncle Miltie and tapped toward him. He was using his walker, as well.

"He's worse today?" Patsy's mother asked. At Gracie's nod, she said, "I'm not surprised. This weather—"

Her brow furrowed, and on an impulse Gracie gave her another hug. "About the money—"

Despite her shrug, Marilyn Clayton sighed.

"We will find it, you know. It's just a matter of time."

A smile tugged at Patsy's mother's lips. "I've visited Nancyalma," she said. "I understand—*totally.*" After a moment, she continued, "And realistically—the bills won't come in until—"

She turned away, and Gracie said with false cheerfulness, "And the money will be found just as surely as Patsy will be safe in God's—and the surgeons'—hands."

Was it only coincidence that the sun slanted through the windows of Abe's Deli the moment the three friends sat down together?

"Look at that!" Amy threw her hands wide. "You brought the sunshine, Mr. Gravino!"

"All by myself?" Rocky asked. "Gracie had nothing to do with it?"

"Careful, there," Abe cautioned.

Sophie stood just behind him, shaking with silent laughter.

"Let Rocky have all the credit," Gracie said magnanimously. "He needs a boost to his ego after yesterday."

"Yesterday?" Amy frowned. "The yard sale?" Smiling at Gracie, she touched her throat, where the choker glistened. "That was the best!"

Sophie crossed her arms. "And what was it you bought, Mr. Gravino, that puts you in such ill repute?"

Rocky spread his hands in a gesture of innocence. "Beats me."

Then, since Rocky seemed totally engrossed in a menu he knew forward and backward anyway, Gracie explained, "It's just that some people of the male persuasion—"

"—think they have certain women figured out?" Rocky interrupted from behind the safety of his menu. "And certain women are upset only because it proved true?"

"Anyone can come up with fifty percent probability." Gracie leaned back in her chair.

"Gotcha!" Abe said softly. "Though I don't know why or how."

Rocky folded his menu. The crinkles in the corners of his eyes deepened. "A bit better than fifty percent, my dear," he said, catching her hand in his. "But suppose we run a small test now, in the presence of unimpeachable witnesses?"

She turned her hand to shake his firmly. "You're on, friend!"

He nodded toward the chalkboard where specials were listed. "Write down your choice. I'll write what I think you'll order. We'll fold the papers and give them to Amy here." He grinned. "If you'll notice, there are five choices, which lowers the probability percentage a bit."

Amy provided pens and two pieces of paper torn from her pad. "This is exciting," she giggled.

"If we were in Cleveland—or in Florida—someone would be taking bets about now."

"But not in Willow Bend," Abe said. "Another thing I like about where I am."

He had said it a bit firmly, Gracie realized—perhaps as a signal to his sister that he still wasn't taking her up on her offer to share a beachfront condominium.

Sophie sniffed and retreated to the kitchen.

Gracie tuned out the remainder of their discourse. What should she order? More importantly, what did Rocky suppose that she'd order? She simply must put this dear but maddening man in his place!

She studied the choices. Stuffed peppers, cabbage rolls, rice pilaf, salmon croquettes, meat loaf.

She simply could not understand why anyone would ever order cabbage rolls as long as any other choice remained. It was one of her least favorite dishes, even when Abe made it his own special way.

Suddenly she knew what she would—what she must—

order. Quickly, she wrote, folded the paper, handed it to Amy ... and prepared to wait.

But Rocky had already turned in his vote. "Let's see." Her expression serious, Amy opened the papers and laid them side by side on the table.

"Both cabbage rolls?" Amy shook her head. "But, Mrs. Parks, I thought you always said—"

"Exactly!" Rocky hooted. "I know this woman well enough to know how stubborn she can be!"

"You win." Gracie shook his hand in surrender.

Amy presented her order pad. "So what do you really want?"

She grimaced. "Cabbage rolls it is."

17

I T'S GOOD, GRACIE TOLD THE LORD—as she and Gooseberry strode along a seldom-traveled road—*to have a moment to breathe.* The yard sale over, no catering assignments until the end of the week—when she'd serve the Historical Society luncheon—and no real obligations for these next two days. All she had to do was to keep things humming along and to enjoy the world around her in the community she was so much a part of.

And oh, yes, help Nancyalma plow through everything left in the house to see if they could finally unearth the elusive auction money.

Visiting Patsy as soon as she was out of surgery and felt like having visitors was on the list, too. *Lord, I know that You're with her at this very moment*—she glanced at her watch. *She'll be anesthetized by now, if they're on schedule. Please give her a hug from me.*

She had to smile at herself. What would a psychiatrist have to say about someone who'd assume such familiarity with God?

Well, a Christian psychiatrist might say, "Right on!" And a secular "shrink" would tell her she was already beyond help.

Of course El, in one of his more cynical moods, had said he'd never known a psychiatrist who didn't need one.

"And how many psychiatrists have you known?" she'd asked.

"Not many." He was so skilled at hedging!

"Would 'not many' be less than twenty?"

"Less than twenty."

"Less than ten?"

He nodded.

This reminded Gracie of Abraham, trying to con God into sparing Sodom and Gomorrah. *You were so patient with him,* she thought now. *As You always are with erring humanity. Certainly more patient than I was with Elmo that day.*

"Less than five?" she'd prodded.

He'd sighed. "Yes, less than five. Less than four. Less than three—"

"Less than one?" But she'd quickly embraced him to show her lack of antagonism.

He turned and returned her embrace, with interest.

"I know, Gracie, that you only want me to not make hasty

generalizations. But any psychiatrist would tell you some-times it can be a harmless tic."

She'd laughed.

They'd laughed together.

Dear Lord, she sighed now, remembering, *how I do miss my dear El!* She stopped just short of asking Him to give El a hug, too.

Gracie and Gooseberry were angling across the church parking lot—perhaps fifteen minutes from ending their walk—when a car veered from the street and pulled up beside them.

Nancyalma's car, Gracie was nearly certain.

But not Nancyalma at the wheel.

"Monty!" she greeted, pretending more enthusiasm than she felt. "And how are you this lovely morning?"

Not meeting her glance, he shrugged. "Not as good as three days from now, when I'm out of this burg."

"Oh. You're leaving so soon?"

"Seems I've been here a year."

"I've never really had the chance to tell you . . ." She continued walking—slowly—but still forcing him to keep up in short spurts of acceleration. "You did a wonderful job as auctioneer. We were all very appreciative."

"Thanks."

Gooseberry broke stride to chase a chipmunk. With some dismay, Gracie watched it take sanctuary somewhere within the church siding. With such an aging building, there was always something to plug, replace or mend, including bolt-holes for tiny creatures.

Gooseberry nosed at the site of disappearance, then found other entertainment. The small drama reminded Gracie vividly of the journal segment Cordelia had shared. Gracie, too, hated to see anything—or anyone—hurt. And if indeed the young writer had been an escaped slave—what added meaning her words evoked.

Monty reclaimed her attention. "Too bad the dough is lost."

"We'll find it—maybe even today!"

He raised an eyebrow. "*We?* Nance didn't say—"

"She forgot to tell you? I'll be over as soon as—"

"No need," he said sharply.

"But I promised—"

"I'll tell her you're busy."

"But I'm not—"

His hand snaked out the window and caught her wrist in a painful grip. "I say you are! Nance's my sister, not yours—and I'll give her all the help she needs." He released her—almost viciously, she thought—and roared away, his tires spinning.

Nancyalma's tires, Gracie corrected herself. And Nancyalma's brother—but a far cry from the personable

Monty-as-auctioneer! Mr. Hyde had been hiding, she realized.

Gooseberry was back, winding around her ankles, his purr as steady as heartbeats, as loud as a tiny unmuffled engine.

"I'm going to help," she told Gooseberry, "no matter what he says. That money's important to all of us. Anyone with a brain of a hickory nut would understand that." She looked to him for confirmation, but Gooseberry merely looked bored.

Uncle Miltie propped his hands on his hips. "I'll go with you. And if that creep tries anything—" He flexed his muscles. "I have moves he's never even heard of."

However, when they arrived at Nancyalma's house, Montgomery X. Montgomery only glowered.

"I thought you'd decided not to come!" Nancyalma wiped her hands on her flowered apron, her face gleaming with sweat and pleasure.

"Not for a moment." Gracie stared back at Monty until he turned away.

"Well!" Uncle Miltie dusted his hands together. "What say me and Gracie start on the bookshelves?"

"Oh! Would you?" Nancyalma might have hugged him if he hadn't been so quick on his feet. "I just can't face them!"

No wonder, Gracie thought. She had seen libraries with fewer volumes. But these bookshelves had never been introduced to amateur organization—much less the Dewey Decimal System or any of its replacements.

"Work from the top down?" Not waiting for an answer, Uncle Miltie tugged down a double handful of dusty books, ranging from the M volume of a 1947 encyclopedia, through an Anya Seton novel, *Halley's Bible Handbook*, *The Little Engine That Could*, a French-English dictionary, a copy of Mark Twain's *Innocents Abroad* and a *Settlement House Cookbook*.

On an impulse, Gracie turned to the page of the encyclopedia where *money* was listed.

No luck.

But the only way to do this, Lord, is to try to think the way Nancyalma might think. She sighed. *But that's a lot like untangling a skein of yarn when a kitten's through with it.*

Uncle Miltie was shaking each volume upside down, fanning the pages—not the best plan for preserving sturdy bindings, but unquestionably efficient.

Gracie began doing the same.

When three shelves were completed, Nancyalma went to get iced tea for all of them.

Montgomery took the occasion to hiss at Gracie, "You didn't listen to me!"

"And don't say you haven't been warned!" Uncle Miltie shot back.

"Here we are!" Nancyalma sang. Her tray clattered with tall glasses, ice cubes and long spoons.

"Ahhh." Uncle Miltie sipped deeply. "Nectar or ambrosia—I never can keep those two straight."

No one bothered to help him out. They were all too busy sipping and swallowing.

Glasses empty, they went back to the search.

Nancyalma was dislodging the cushions from a love-seat. "Even though I've done this twice before," she said, her voice defeated.

"Fourth shelf down!" Uncle Miltie announced. "Looks like a lot of different songbooks—mostly hymns."

"*That's it!*" Nancyalma tripped over one of the cushions and sat down suddenly. Uncle Miltie continued tugging, and Gracie stood open-mouthed as several hymnals spilled bills like autumn leaves.

Nancyalma sighed happily. "I *knew* I'd put it somewhere that made sense!"

"To you, maybe," Monty muttered—leaving his post to gather up a few volumes.

But Gracie understood. Hymnbook . . . choir. *Don't tell me I'm beginning to think like Nancyalma! Well, it does make sense . . . in a way.*

As the heap of books and bills grew, there was no time for worrying whether the choice of hiding place was a logical one or not. At last, all the hymnbooks were emptied. Uncle Miltie stacked them in neat piles while the other three stuffed money in a box Nancyalma produced. At one particular moment, as Gracie turned, she suspected that Monty had stuffed some bills in his pocket.

"Head cold," he said gruffly, and carefully extracted a crumpled handkerchief.

Now what, Lord? she asked, not sure which course to take. *Just how will it be best to handle this?*

Of course! The total receipts had been tallied the day of the auction. "Let's count to be certain we have it all," she suggested off-handedly.

"Waste of time," Monty grumbled. "Whatever there is, there is."

"No, really, dear," Nancyalma urged. "Remember how I lose things ... what if I did something really stupid?"

Uncle Miltie rolled his eyes in Gracie's direction, as Nancyalma began stacking bills by denomination. As they worked, Gracie remembered, "There was some change ..."

"Oh, yes!" Nancyalma chirped. "It's safe; now I remember everything. I put it in a hamper."

"A ... hamper?" Uncle Miltie shook his head.

"That was an easy one to remember. Hampers ... changing clothes ... change—I'll go get it."

When the count was complete, it was nearly six hundred dollars short. "How *could* it be?" Nancyalma worried, and Gracie thought Monty looked increasingly uncomfortable. *Didn't he realize we'd have counted it, Lord? But I can't just say, "Empty your pockets, why don't you, Montgomery X. Montgomery, you thief."*

"We've got to find it!" Nancyalma pushed back her chair. "We've absolutely got to find it! Even," she finished firmly, "if it means ripping the house apart!"

Monty sighed. "Let me go check, Nance. We might just have missed . . . a hymnal, or something. You three wait here—and relax." Mopping his forehead, he took off at a near-sprint.

It was only moments when he returned, a sheaf of bills in his hand. "Guess what," he sighed. "I was right."

"Dear Monty!" His sister hugged him. "Thank you!"

"Which book was it in?" Uncle Miltie asked dryly.

Monty looked startled. "I . . . forgot to notice. . . ."

"Just so it's found—that's all that matters. Right, Gracie?"

"Uh, yes. Of course. And I'll be happy to take it to the bank for you. Right now."

Uncle Miltie gave her a "good move" signal, Nancyalma smiled her gratitude and Monty slumped into a chair.

"I was going to—" he began.

Nancyalma patted his hand. "I wouldn't think of it, dear! You've been *such* a help—and you haven't even begun to pack!" She turned to Gracie. "I'll put it all into a grocery bag. And get you a deposit slip."

"And I'll go with you," Uncle Miltie said. "Just in case there are any stagecoach robbers out there."

18

PATSY LOOKED MINUTE in her swathing of sheets and surrounded by an entire village of stuffed animals. At the moment, she was in traction. Her face, though pale and strained, wreathed itself in smiles. "Mrs. Parks! You came to see me! And Mr. Morgan! And Mr. Gravino!"

"Take it easy, young lady," Uncle Miltie warned, smiling. From behind his back he drew a large plush cat.

"Just like Gooseberry!" she cried, "except Gooseberry's not blue!" She hugged the toy, nearly as big as she, her eyes widening even further as Rocky made his offering, a beautifully illustrated book of Bible stories for children.

Is it significant, Lord, Gracie asked, *that Rocky chose a Christian book even though he conveys indifference?*

But Rocky was saying, "I looked at a lot of other books, but thought you'd like this one."

Patsy looked expectantly to Gracie.

"Guess," Gracie said.

"Now, let me see." Patsy adopted a mode of concentration. "What could it be, I wonder?" She closed her eyes, as though divining. "I see . . . I see . . . chocolate chip cookies!"

They were all laughing when Patsy's mother entered the room.

Gracie could tell at a glance that this surgery was still not the final answer to Patsy's problem.

But it wasn't until they had gone quietly from the room that another thought struck. Of all the flowers, cards and gifts filling every available space of windowsill, table and bed—there had been no carved wax animal.

How could the carver—who had commemorated far lesser crises with his or her thoughtful gifts—possibly neglect little Patsy?

Gracie made two other quick visits during Patsy's hospital stay. She would be home soon.

"It's only a matter of time," Uncle Miltie grumbled, "before we have drive-by brain surgery. Like ordering 'to go' at a burger joint."

Gracie laughed. She had often felt indignant at the thought of surgery patients released long before mobility had returned, not to mention brand-new mothers sent home too exhausted to enjoy their tiny blessings.

"I'll be in a wheelchair for a while," Patsy said, eyes shining. "It's going to have purple streamers on the back!"

"Wow!" Uncle Miltie said, his voice not quite as hearty, Gracie suspected, as he'd planned. "Imagine, a purple chariot."

"No, just the streamers will be purple."

"We could paint the rest."

Patsy giggled. "I don't think they'd like that!"

"Can't never tell." Uncle Miltie wagged a finger. "You just can't never tell."

Later, in the parking lot, he said, "I wanted to tell some jokes—cheer her up, you know. But Gracie, I just didn't feel in a joking mood. Poor, poor little tyke!"

Two days after Patsy was to come home, Gracie was up to her eyebrows in preparations for the Historical Society luncheon. She was in the midst of rolling dough when Cordelia Fountain stopped by, wearing jeans and a floppy straw hat. Today her only nod to the past was a T-shirt she'd bought years ago at Gettysburg.

"I'm a nervous wreck!" she said. "Those biscuits look good, Gracie, but then they always do. Although—" She perched on the stool like a dragonfly eager to be off again. "Are you having anything that evokes the Civil War?"

Gracie reached past her to get the maraschino cherries. "What did you have in mind? Grits?"

Cordelia shuddered delicately. "How did they ever abide those? My one cousin has them for breakfast every morning, with a soft-boiled egg." Another shudder. "I'd sooner starve."

"Grits!" Uncle Miltie barged through the screen door. "I heard that. Poor excuse for a starch is all I can say!"

Gracie laughed.

He continued, "Ever hear about the waitress who asked the customer, 'Wanna roll?' And when the customer said 'Sure,' she said, 'Well, roll in the parking lot. We just had the carpet cleaned.'"

Cordelia groaned.

"Thought you'd like it!" Uncle Miltie exulted. "Do you need me for anything, my dear?"

"I need you to take a nap in the hammock," Gracie suggested.

"I could do that!" He pushed his face against the screen. "But what you're really doing is keeping me away from the Hysterical Society's food." He grinned at Cordelia.

"I do so admire you." Cordelia settled back at last. "How you can bake and deal with his jokes all at the same time."

And also put up with unexpected company, Gracie thought. But she just smiled pleasantly and circumnavigated Cordelia to get to the spice cabinet.

Mid-afternoon, needing a break, Gracie decided to take a

short walk—just to enjoy the air and the scents of early autumn. Gooseberry elected to accompany her.

It seemed each day she could see more brilliance in the foliage, could feel a bit more briskness in the air. "Won't be long, Gooseberry," she confided, "and we'll be wading through snow. And I don't mind a bit. But don't tell Uncle Miltie."

She switched over to God. *You send the seasons in their order, as it says in—is it Ecclesiastes? And each has its own splendors. I'll admit, there are times in March when I think we've had more than enough ice and snow—but there are times in the summer when I get tired of melting in the heat. It's just the nature of your highest creations, I guess, to need something to complain about. But, Lord—we can't even begin to comprehend the complexity, the completeness of Your creations! Who but You would have thought of putting that tiny little purple flower among all those minuscule white ones that make up Queen Anne's lace? That flower alone is enough to prove Your existence!*

Gooseberry interrupted her thought by stopping in front of her foot and stiffening. She could sense his hackles rising as they did for only one person.

Sure enough, there was Barry Benton, tossing his tennis ball against a fence—bang! Bang! Bang! Bang!

But—left-handed! His right arm hung in a sling fastened on his left shoulder.

"Barry!" she called, expecting him to acknowledge her with a sulky grunt, if at all.

She nearly collapsed when he turned with a smile and a cheery, "Hi, Mrs. Parks!"

"What happened to you?" She hoped he'd think she meant the sling—though she was more amazed by the improvement in attitude.

"Broke my collarbone fixing a window somebody broke."

Bang! Bang! Bang!

"At the boutique?"

"Yeah. She thought I did it, but I didn't. It was my ball, though."

"Then it was wonderful that you fixed it."

"Yeah. I wanted the ball back."

"And your collarbone?"

"Fell. The ladder wasn't set straight." He threw the ball one last time, caught it deftly and gave her his total attention. "Gotta get back to school, soon. I had an excuse to see the bone doctor."

He was a nice-looking boy, when he wasn't scowling, Gracie realized. How could it be that a broken collarbone seemed to agree with him? She decided to ask him if he'd like to come to her house for some chocolate chip cookies and milk.

His face lit up. "I always envied the other kids when you

baked them stuff." He looked down, his voice lowering, as well. "It's no wonder you never asked me before. I've been a real—"

He swallowed audibly, giving her opportunity to fill in a number of descriptive nouns. Only mentally, of course.

But what had changed him?

He stooped to retrieve something resting in the grass.

It was a wax carving of a fish. With a wick.

Tears smarted in her eyes. *Can one small gift of comfort effect such a total turnaround? If it comes with Your blessing, then I feel it can.*

Oh, how she hoped it had!

*"'The proof is in the pudding,'" Uncle Miltie quoted as she recited Barry Benton's amazing transformation. "Or, more to the point, the cookies. How many did you give him?"

"Not as many as I gave you." She carried another load of salads to the van.

"I should hope not! If that ratio ever changes, I'll take up sulking."

She laughed. "And throwing baseballs through windows," she added, "though he insists he didn't break Marge's."

"That woman! Wouldn't surprise me if a cuckoo flew in. 'Birds of a feather,' you know."

Gracie didn't respond. In the first place, he'd turn a deaf

ear. In the second—she knew that he had a soft spot in his heart for Marge, whatever he said.

Anyway, thank You, Lord, for Barry's transformation—he has done some growing on his own, and You must have opened his heart, as well.

A sudden thought stopped her in her tracks.

Uncle Miltie braked his walker just short of collision. "What's wrong, Gracie? Stung by a bee?"

"No," she answered thoughtfully, "by a bolt of lightning, I expect."

It had just occurred to her that the last time she'd prayed about Barry, she'd petitioned God to bring him to his senses.

Whispering another quick *thank You,* she continued packing for the luncheon.

Gracie had been invited several times, but had never joined the Historical Society. Even though she catered many of their luncheons and parties, she was particularly glad she was serving rather than required to sit on a folding chair juggling a cup of hot tea and a small plate of cookies. Making small talk was what she found most difficult of all.

"I love socializing!" Marge had said many times. And since she had joined the Society when asked, she was in attendance today as a guest rather than as Gracie's right-hand woman.

"It doesn't feel quite right," she confided, patting her coiffure which did, indeed, Gracie thought, look historical—though she'd have been hard-put to say from what era.

"Daydreaming?" Marge teased.

"Admiring your striped dress. It's so cheerful."

Marge swirled around. "It's one of my favorites, too."

Uncle Miltie was there to bring her back to earth. "Puts me in mind of a lady convict."

They stared him down simultaneously.

Gracie was a bit concerned about Cordelia, who seemed now even more flustered than she had on her visit a few days earlier. Her color was high enough to suggest an imminent stroke, and she seemed to struggle for breath. "Oh, Gracie," she sighed on one of her many non-essential visits to the kitchen, "I'll just die if the reporter doesn't get here from Chicago!"

Gracie barely saved a relish dish. *"Chicago?"*

Cordelia shrugged. "Such a significant story deserves broader coverage than it's likely to get—" she glanced warily at Gracie, "—around here."

Gracie knew that Rocky, always badgered by Cordelia for greater coverage in the paper, had adopted a "wait and see" approach. But now—a Chicago reporter? Gracie hoped that Mrs. Fountain hadn't—as Uncle Miltie might put it—"bitten off more than she could chew."

THE REPORTER, AMANDA BLAKE, was in her early
forties, her auburn hair tugged back in a severe bun
that would have straightened out the wrinkles in her forehead, Gracie was certain, had there been any. Her suit was
severe as well: black herring-bone, with a white-dotted ascot.
Horn-rimmed glasses rode the bridge of her delicate nose.
Her eyes were cucumber-green, her lipstick cinnamon color—
fingernails painted to match—and her smile the widest and
whitest Gracie had ever seen.

She was beautiful

And she was not unknown to everyone in the room.
Several puzzled for a moment, then shrugged and turned
away. But when Cordelia said proudly, "Ladies, I'd like to
introduce—" Marybeth Bower burst out, "Mandy! Mandy
Petrucci—is it really you?"

Apparently it was.

Cordelia, firmly upstaged, stood to one side.

When the furor quieted, Mandy Petrucci-now-Blake addressed the group.

"When I heard about this story—when Ms. Fountain called our women's editor—I wondered if I knew the house she meant. Years ago—thirty, by now—I spent most of the summer here. Next door to Ms. Fountain's was a girl—"

"Sylvia!" Marybeth supplied.

"Sylvia." Mandy smiled. "It was the best summer of my life—well, at least until I met my husband."

Laughter rippled.

"But am I keeping you from your business—or, worse yet, your food? Will everything cold get warm? And everything hot grow cold?"

Gracie assured her that the food would be fine.

"I'll be as brief as possible." Mandy took a seat, and everyone else followed suit. Everyone, that is, except Gracie and Uncle Miltie, who tried to make themselves invisible. Mandy continued thoughtfully, "Sylvia had such an imagination! She knew there was a secret room next door. Where runaway slaves had once been harbored.

"No one seemed to care much then. No one but us." Mandy smiled. "We would play dress up and pretend that we lived a hundred years earlier. We even turned *Gone With the Wind* into a ballet!"

Marybeth smiled.

"We had no idea we were stomping and shrieking in such an historic place! Oh—and out by the old springhouse!" Mandy paused. "That's where we buried Sylvia's cat."

Stark silence fell.

No one moved. No one stirred.

And then Cordelia asked, "Her cat?"

Mandy seemed oblivious to Cordelia's shock. "He was a caramel-colored stray, but we all loved him dearly. Remember, Marybeth? We couldn't decide whether to call him Honey, Caramel or Butterscotch."

Marybeth nodded. "But I didn't know about the spring-house. And I didn't realize the cat had died. By the time we came back from our summer vacation, you and Sylvia were both gone. And I guess I assumed—"

"Of course! Why wouldn't you? Poor Butterscotch. We wrapped him in an old scrap of blanket we'd found in Sylvia's attic."

Several women exchanged knowing glances.

"And the journal—"

"The journal! You found that, too!" Mandy was on her feet. "Where? May I see it? Sylvia's handwriting left a lot to be desired, but she insisted on being our dramatist and record-keeper."

She paused, startled. "Oh, Ms. Fountain! Is that *the* journal? . . . And our Butterscotch the skeleton? . . . And you thought— Oh, I'm so, so sorry!"

Someone had to do something to salvage the situation, and Gracie sensed that she was that "someone."

"If you'll find your places," she invited, "we'll begin to serve. Mrs. Blake, as our guest, would you please offer thanks?"

It was another Sunday. Rocky, Abe and Gracie sat at their usual table. Abe contemplated the meanderings of a ladybug, who apparently had picked the deli as a nice place to spend the winter.

There seemed little doubt that autumn was waning. A frost had taken all but the hardiest marigolds. Leaves—colorful, curled and brittle—littered the streets and sidewalks. Gracie's morning praise-walks required a sweatshirt—at least until her pace had warmed her.

Rocky said, "Well things turned out rather well, all things considered."

"That was a nice human interest story Mandy Blake wrote."

"A lovely spread," Rocky agreed. "The picture of Cordelia was a bit blurry, maybe—but a nice approach. Reminiscence. Nostalgia. And I guess you'd say closure."

"Cordelia was quite pleased, considering everything."

"And here? Is Sophie leaving this week? We'll soon be nostalgic for her baking!"

Abe smiled, "Like the geese, the ducks and the starlings, my sister is flying to her southern nest. I believe she has already packed."

"And our carver," Rocky said. "I believe he or she left a token for Cordelia."

"A turtle." Gracie had seen it when she stopped by for a visit. Cordelia had placed it in the china closet on the shelf vacated by the remains of the late Butterscotch—now decently interred—and the journal, now in Mandy's delighted possession. "I wonder who that is. The carver."

Amy had been standing quietly, listening. "I have no idea who—but I do know that those unexpected little gifts are as good as any hug."

"I wonder if we'll ever know," Gracie said softly.

"But now!" Suddenly Abe was the brisk businessman. "I wonder, my dear Mrs. Parks, could I interest you in a large helping of cabbage roll?"

Lord, we are so blessed with friends. It was Monday morning, and frost clung to every blade of grass, to every twig. Soon the sun would liquify its crystals, and the beauty would be lost. *I would have hated to sleep late, Lord . . . to have missed this. Or I might have been tarrying over a cup of coffee and the newspaper. How many glorious mornings, I wonder, have You created without our noticing?*

Now, for the moment, only one mystery remains. The carver who leaves small love tokens. Give us the grace to accept such gifts without probing for the giver's identity.

She was nearly home. She had been bending God's ear for most of her walk.

Uncle Miltie beckoned her in, and shut the door immediately behind her. "Not fit for an Eskimo to be out," he grumped. "And we have company." He nodded toward the living room.

Patsy perched primly on the seat of her little wheelchair, Gooseberry draped across her lap. Her purple streamers hung limp. "It's my first day out all alone," she said, "and I wanted to come here first of all."

"We're honored!" Uncle Miltie said loudly, and explained to Gracie, "Marilyn went to do some shopping while we visit."

"This calls for a celebration!" Gracie went to the kitchen for some snickerdoodles and ice cream.

They spoke of many things—but not of the hospital. Not of the failed surgery. Not even of how long it might be before the wheelchair could be discarded in favor of the familiar walker.

"I've been wondering." Patsy scraped her bowl and seemed to consider licking it. "Does anybody know yet . . . who the non-a-muss carver is?"

"We were talking about that just yesterday," Gracie said—then stopped. *Non-a-muss. NAMS.* Could it be? This child? In the beginning, someone had mentioned the Grandma Moses-like simplicity. . . .

Patsy looked up, her eyes wide and guileless. Her breath seemed suspended.

Gracie made her decision easily. "No. No one seems to have a clue. I have a feeling we may never know."

Stroking Gooseberry, Patsy smiled.

Gracie's Mellow Chili

- ✓ 1 pound extra lean ground beef
- ✓ One 15 1/2 ounce can dark red kidney beans, rinsed and drained
- ✓ One 15 1/2 ounce can pinto beans, rinsed and drained
- ✓ One 15 1/2 ounce can pink beans, rinsed and drained
- ✓ One 8 ounce can stewed tomatoes
- ✓ One 28 ounce can Italian plum tomatoes, chopped
- ✓ One 8 ounce can tomato sauce
- ✓ 1 small onion
- ✓ 2 cloves garlic
- ✓ 3 tablespoons chili powder, or to taste
- ✓ 1/2 teaspoon ground cumin
- ✓ 1 teaspoon paprika
- ✓ 1 teaspoon oregano
- ✓ 1 teaspoon dried mustard
- ✓ 1 tablespoon Dijon-style mustard
- ✓ 2 tablespoons wine vinegar
- ✓ 2 small bay leaves
- Dried cherries (optional)
- Salt and pepper as needed

Brown the meat and drain off excess fat. Put meat in heavy cooking pot with beans, tomatoes and tomato sauce. Cook uncovered, stirring occasionally, for ten minutes. Chop onion and garlic finely, and sauté until translucent, then add to pot. Add spices, mustard, vinegar and bay leaves. Cover and simmer chili mix over low heat until well thickened—this could take one hour to one-and-a-half hours. Serve either the bare-bones way, with saltine crackers and chunks of cheddar, or allow chili eaters to help themselves to a variety of toppings (chopped green and red peppers, sour cream, avocado slices, shredded cheddar, cut-up scallions or onion, tomato salsa, etc.).

Says Gracie, "One afternoon, just as I was getting ready to make dinner, I noticed a small half-bag of dried cherries in the fridge. I soaked them in water, threw them into the simmering chili and found, after it had all cooked down into a delicious stew, that 'cherry chili' was a real discovery. The only problem is, I'd never call it that, for fear of putting Uncle Miltie off before he even tasted it!"

About the Author

In the Minshull household, bookcases overflow, huddled tropical plants compete for light, niches hold office equipment, and most flat surfaces yield to milk glass, assorted curios for writing workshops and various works-in-progress.

"Where I go, clutter happens," admits Evelyn, author of twenty-plus published books, erstwhile artist, compulsive teacher, gardener, baker-of-cookies and knitter-of-booties she gives away—often to strangers.

Every Sunday, spring through fall, she takes flowers to church. It's a habit, a ministry, continued in her mother's memory. "Mother taught a reverence for words. My father encouraged my art. But Freddie and our three daughters not only survived my clutter, they participated in a multitude of crafts and puppet performances that grew from it. And the girls were my best literary critics—ever."

Valerie, Melanie and Robin are grown and gone now, living in Kentucky, North Carolina and central Pennsylvania. Granddaughter Micky attends Vanderbilt University. Grandsons Jonathan and Benjamin are in elementary school. Fred, husband and unflagging encourager, is still stepping casually around piles of books.

Fred built their ranch-style home on three acres of former apple orchard and sheep pasture. Twelve flowerbeds (so far) interrupt the flow of lawn. Pennsylvania white-tailed deer, enticed by fallen apples, venture from the lower half-acre, once a pasture for the daughters' horses but now a tangle of shrubs and lofty oaks.

"This is my favorite place on earth," Evelyn says.

Fred smiles.